FORGOTTEN BEAST

C M RAYNE

FORGOTTEN BEAST

THE THIRD BOOK IN THE ANDARA SERIES

Adam Scythe drew the pictures

dancing paper

This is a work of fiction. Names, characters, businesses, places, events and incidents are either the products of the author's imagination or used in a fictitious manner. Any resemblance to actual persons, living or dead, or actual events is purely coincidental.

FORGOTTEN BEAST

Published by Dancing Paper
Copyright © 2017 by C.M. Rayne
Cover art and illustrations by Adam Scythe
Constellation font by Marianela Grande

ISBN 978-615-80463-2-9

www.cmrayne.com

To the one who embraces me, darkness and all.

"Judge tenderly, if you must. There is usually a side you have not heard, a story you know nothing about, and a battle waged that you are not having to fight."

Traci Lea LaRussa

1 THE NOT SO ORDINARY BOY

Regina screamed when she woke up in the middle of the night. Someone was in her hut again. It was not someone who had a tendency to wake her up in the middle of the night, like Jasper or the Oracle; it was not even someone less threatening, like Joey or Pyro.

A new face was staring at Regina. A boy, who must have been a couple of years older than her. His hair was brown and shaggy, his clothes looked like hand-me-downs, oversized on him. But Regina didn't notice any of these attributes—they were not what made her scream.

Admittedly, this boy was not the best person to wake a stranger up in the middle of the night. Not that it was pleasant to wake up to any stranger in one's house, but this particular boy was not an ordinary person at all. Not on the outside, at least.

Now, Regina White was not a girl who would judge anyone based on their appearance. But even the best person would scream if they got woken up by a stranger touching their cheeks in the middle of the night—especially if that stranger's face was not like an average person's.

Regina was fully awake in a matter of seconds. She felt bad for screaming. But then she remembered that no matter what this boy's face looked like, he was still a stranger. In her hut. In the middle of the night.

"Who—who are you?" Regina noticed Brunorth sitting in the middle of the room, watching the intruder, his head tilted to the side. This made Regina relax a bit. The dragon was not fond of people who had any intention to hurt her.

The boy, who had taken a few steps back when Regina screamed in his face, was watching her with wide eyes.

It was not a comfortable situation.

The boy looked away and scratched his head. Regina now noticed his clothes, which hung on him like someone five times bigger had stretched them out.

"I'm not sure." The boy's voice was soft like butter. It made Regina's shoulders relax even more.

"What do you mean, you're not sure?" Regina lowered the white duvet, which she had pulled up to hide the bottom half of her face. "What's your name?"

The boy looked at Regina like she had just asked the most difficult question in the world.

Suddenly, Regina started to think that the outside of this boy was not the only part of him that wasn't ordinary. She placed her bare feet on the floor.

"Do you know why you were touching my face? Why you came in here? This is my hut, you know." Regina tried to speak as gently as she could.

"I know that." The boy's voice rang with annoyance. "Just because I don't remember my name or who I am or, you know . . . anything for that matter, doesn't mean I'm stupid." He crossed his arms. "Agnitio brought me here." His voice was calmer now. "I was on my way to my hut when I walked past this hut and . . . saw you."

Regina's nose wrinkled just a tiny bit. "You watched me sleep?"

"It's not . . . like that. I don't . . . know." His head hung low. "I felt like . . . I knew you. Don't we know each other? From somewhere?"

11

Regina shook her head.

"Too bad. I was hoping you could tell me more about myself than what I seem to know."

"You don't remember anything?"

"No. I just remember a faun showing up at the side of my bed and bringing me here. I chose a hut, and after that I saw you. And now I'm here. That's all I know basically."

From the way the boy was speaking, it was clear he had no issues on the inside.

"Oh, and this." He gestured toward his own face. "I remember that I was born like this. No accidents or anything. Sorry if I scared you, by the way. I tend to do that to people. I assume." He smiled. And the large patch of skin around his right eye that looked like chewed up bubble gum didn't seem as scary when he did.

Regina noticed something else in his eyes now. The way he looked at her—it was more than a stranger looking at a stranger. She felt safe under his gaze.

"So, you came in here because you thought you knew me?" Regina pulled up her shoulders.

"Yeah, I mean"—he shrugged—"are you sure we don't?" He looked at Regina with squinted eyes. "I still feel like we do."

"Well, I do tend to forget some memories." Regina raised her brows. "But, no, I think I would remember you."

The boy nodded. His look made it obvious he didn't yet accept that he and Regina didn't know each other.

Regina doubted many things about herself, but this time, she was sure she had never met the boy standing in front of her. That face and that gaze was not something she would have forgotten.

The boy turned and noticed Brunorth. "Oh, wow. A dragon," he said with not that big of a surprise. He crouched down and petted Brunorth, who rolled on his back like a happy dog. "I like you." He laughed. "Our faces are kind of similar. Don't you think?" He looked at Regina.

Regina smiled. What had caused her to scream a short while ago didn't seem like such a big deal now.

"Yeah, you're right," Regina said with a smile. "You might be half dragon."

The boy laughed. "Who knows? I hope I am."

Regina watched him pet Brunorth for a long moment. She had only met this boy a few minutes ago, but during those intense minutes, she had already grown to like him.

Coming to Andara was a scary experience on its own, she couldn't even imagine what it must have been like with absolutely no memories.

"So basically," Regina said, musing, "Agnitio was the first person you saw. The only person. So, did you think the world was inhabited by faun people?"

The boy laughed again. His voice became more and more carefree. "No," he said, raising his brows. "I have a general knowledge about the world. I just don't have memories. About my own life, you know."

Brunorth began making a sound that was closest to a cat's purring as he petted his stomach.

"Oh, okay." Regina nodded and felt a little stupid, even though she had asked that question as a half-joke.

The boy stood up and looked at Regina. His eyes were serious, but never lacking their protective quality. Regina could have snuggled up in his look as if it were a warm blanket.

The plant called Dragontears that had grown all over the walls of the hut lit up the room with the warm light of its small buds. Everything was quiet and serene.

"So, are you okay?" asked the boy, the warm light

softening his face. "Are you doing okay?"

Regina didn't know why he was asking her such a question, but she nodded.

"They aren't mean to you?"

"Mean?" Regina asked, confused. "No." She shook her head. "Who?"

The boy looked at her, his eyes jumping from left to right between hers. He was searching for an answer he couldn't find.

"I don't know," he said finally. "I just felt like I needed to ask."

"I'm okay." Regina stood up. "I'm so okay, that I'm going to help you."

"What do you mean? How?"

"Agnitio. He knows everything. I'm sure he could tell you who you are." Regina made her way toward the wardrobe, which contained the exact same items her wardrobe back home did, and began picking out pieces from the large pile of clothes.

"We can ask him questions? I didn't know that. He said that I can find answers if I journey through this land or something like that."

Regina waved her hand. "I'm sure he will tell you *something*. He's a nice guy. We're friends. I'm sure he'll help you."

The boy shrugged. "Okay, worth a try. I'm not sleepy anyway. Are you?"

"No, it's okay. I'm up now." Shielded by the large doors of the wardrobe, Regina got dressed as quickly as she could. When she was done and closed the doors, she saw that the boy was facing away from her. He had probably turned away on purpose.

"Let's go," Regina said as she passed him on her way to the door.

The boy stood in front of Regina and looked down at her. He swept the hair out of Regina's face. "If you're sleepy, tell me immediately, okay? I will bring you right back." His voice was impossibly soft and gentle.

Regina looked at him for a moment, not knowing how to react. She took a step back. "Thanks, but Agnitio's hut is not that far away."

The boy shook his head like he was trying to shake something off. "Sorry, yeah," he said, not looking at Regina and turning toward the door.

As he opened the door and exited the hut, Regina heard him mumble, "We don't know each other." He sounded like he was trying to convince himself.

2: NOT QUITE BLACK, NOT QUITE WHITE

Regina and the mysterious boy made their way across the Field of Cetana. The night covered the land like a soft blanket—all was quiet and calm. Only the sound of their feet and Brunorth's legs rustled in the silence.

The millions of stars above them lit up the whole field. The other huts glowed from the inside like lanterns across the land.

Regina wasn't tired. Even though she often didn't sleep through the night in Andara, she was never fatigued. Probably one of the perks of time standing still.

"Is Agnitio up?" Regina wondered aloud. She wasn't sure if the faun ever slept at all.

"He just brought me here not that long ago. So I assume he is."

Regina sneaked a peek at the boy. The light of the stars glinted on his face. Even under the shadow of the night, his eyes glowed with blueness. It was strange—to see such beautiful eyes under such . . . unusual skin. Even in her mind, Regina didn't want to think about the boy as "imperfect" or "flawed." Who knew what "perfect" was, anyway?

The boy noticed she was staring. Regina tore her eyes away, but she still saw him smiling.

"It's okay, little one, I don't mind. You have to get used to it, I know."

"It's not that, I just . . ." Regina tried to explain herself, but she couldn't possibly say that she was looking at his beautiful eyes or any other part of his "unusual" face, so she just stayed quiet instead of finishing her sentence.

Before she could get embarrassed because of her awkward silence, her eyes jumped to something next to the boy. It was like a sudden apparition walking beside him—a black dog . . . skeleton?

But like a flickering light, it was gone as fast as it had appeared. Regina rubbed her eyes, blinked a couple of times and checked again—nothing was there. *It was probably just the darkness and the light of the stars playing tricks on my eyes*, she thought and left it at that.

Agnitio's hut was only a couple of steps away, but before they could reach it and consider knocking on his door in the middle of the night, a voice sounded behind them, startling them so much that they immediately stopped in their steps.

"The stars are especially bright tonight."

Regina and the boy turned around, and they looked right at Agnitio. The faun stood with hands relaxed behind his back, looking up at the stars with a smile.

"It's always nice to do nothing and just appreciate the beauty of this world." He sighed like he had just gotten up from the most relaxing sleep then looked at Regina and the boy with a smile. "I'm glad you came. I'm always available. Even during the night. Fauns don't need much sleep." He started toward his hut. "Nangrass tea?" he asked, turning back from the doorway.

"Sure, thank you." Regina nodded encouragingly at the boy. "You should try it, it's great."

They sat at Agnitio's old wooden table. His hut had a peculiar scent that Regina couldn't quite put her finger on. But if she had to, she would have said that it smelled like home.

The dozens, maybe hundreds of random objects Agnitio kept on his shelves gave the space a particular vibe. Regina knew every single item carried a choice once made. Jasper's teddy bear and her bracelet were both somewhere on those shelves as well. All these objects made Regina feel a comforting sense of balance. Like no wrong could ever be without a right.

"So, Mal, Regina, what can I help you with on this fine night?" The faun asked as he prepared them some tea.

"Mal, you mean my name is Mal?" The boy asked with wide eyes. "That can't be my full name, right?"

Regina looked between Agnitio and the boy. She hadn't expected to get information this easily.

Agnitio turned toward them, the jar with the sleeping Nangrass root in his hand. "It's not your full name, indeed. But what's in a name, anyway?" He tilted his head, the goat horns on it glinting in the light of the Dragontears. "It's all you need to know, trust me."

Regina looked at Mal with raised brows and a smile. It was a start.

"Mal." Mal let the taste of his name linger in his mouth.

21

"Could you tell me a bit more about me? I don't really remember much. Anything, actually."

"Yes, Mal, I know." Agnitio rested his eyes on Mal, probably contemplating what he should say and what he shouldn't say. "You will remember in due time." He turned back toward the kitchen. "I have to confess, I wouldn't have thought you would bump into Regina. There are so many people here. Your encounter was very . . . unlikely."

"I noticed her from . . . her window." Mal lowered his head. He was embarrassed, maybe even a little ashamed.

"From her window, huh?" Agnitio turned back toward them, now stirring a cup of tea. "Interesting. It's almost like, you couldn't *not* notice her, isn't it?"

Mal shrugged. "I guess. I feel like we know each other. She insists we don't, but I don't know."

"Yes." Agnitio stirred the tea unaffected, like what Mal had said was obvious.

"Do we know each other?" asked Regina. "I could have forgotten . . ."

"I know you had a repressed memory before, Regina, but people only forget what they don't want to remember. At your age, at least."

"I guess that means we really don't know each other," Regina said, turning toward Mal.

Mal didn't reply, and Regina couldn't help but feel that he still didn't believe the two of them were strangers.

Agnitio placed two cups of tea in front of them and one in front of himself. He sat down across the table from them.

Regina watched the liquid swirl and twirl from translucent to a sparkling shade somewhere between purple and pink. She smiled at the thought that the empathetic Nangrass tea chose that color to represent her in that moment.

"It's not quite purple, not quite pink. What color did you get?" she asked, looking at Mal, who was staring at her without blinking.

"Not quite purple, not quite pink," he said quietly, zoned out. "Ness . . ."

"Excuse me?" said Regina.

"Your name should be Ness. Not Regina." Mal started blinking now, and he looked at Regina with clear eyes again.

"Ness? Like the monster?" Regina laughed. "No one has ever called me that before. Regina, Reg, Reggie maybe." She leaned toward Mal's cup to check what color it had changed to, but when she saw it, she could only say, "Oh."

Mal's tea looked more like a chocolate and vanilla swirl—half of it black, half of it white, the beverage almost seemed like it didn't know what color to choose from the two.

"That's weird." Regina turned toward Agnitio. "Isn't it?"

Agnitio rested his gaze on Mal's tea. "Well, *I'm* not surprised," he said with a smile.

Mal seemed a bit unnerved as he stared at his tea.

"You can drink it," Agnitio said softly. "It helps."

They all drank their beverages. As usual, it tasted wonderful. Sweet, but not too sweet, like strawberry cream, Regina's favorite.

"So, you really won't tell me anything?" Mal asked after he placed his empty cup on the table.

"I will tell you one thing. What you have here, Mal, is a rare opportunity not available to most. You don't remember who you were, so you are free to choose who to be. Take advantage of it. And once you make that decision, never let it go, not even when the memories come knocking."

Mal looked at Agnitio, considering his words. "Okay, Agnitio, thank you," he said finally and stood up from his chair, ready to leave.

"I believe in you, Mal. And I'm always here if you need me." Agnitio stood up from his chair as well. He looked at Mal with a smile.

Mal nodded and turned around then exited the hut. "Thanks for the weird tea. It was really good," he said from the door. "I'll come back to drink another one once I'm done with my journey."

Agnitio nodded. "I hope you will."

After Mal went out the door, Regina stood up too, thanked the faun for the tea and started toward the door. She stopped when she felt Agnitio's hand on her shoulder.

"Regina," said the faun, "there's something I want to tell you."

Regina turned around to face him. Despite the weight of his words, Agnitio didn't look distressed at all. Just like always, Regina felt like everything was going to be all right when she looked at him.

"Mal's situation is quite special. I know you are aware of that. But what you might not be aware of is the importance of who *you* are next to him. And who everybody else is who meets him." Agnitio placed his hands behind his back. "You have a chance to save more than one life. But you shouldn't be burdened. You will do just fine without all those thoughts swirling in your head." Agnitio smiled.

"Um, okay." Regina blinked with wide eyes a couple of times. "I'll try my best, Agnitio."

"I know you will."

With that, Regina turned around and left the hut. Despite what Agnitio had said, thoughts swirled around like mad inside of her head, of course.

When Mal looked at her with a smile, she didn't know what to do or say. Who she was next to him was crucial, after all. Lives depended on it, apparently.

Regina didn't even notice that the sun had come up while they had been inside Agnitio's hut.

"Hey, Regina, what are you doing here?" Joey's voice danced into her right ear. And Joey's voice, she was always glad to hear. She felt his hand on her shoulder.

But before she could turn to look at the raven-haired boy, greet him, smile at him, a violent blow forced itself between Regina and Joey.

"Don't touch her!" Mal's voice shook with rage.

When Regina managed to turn her head, Joey was already on the ground.

3. UNWANTED PROTECTOR

"What are you doing, Mal?" Regina pushed Mal aside from in front of her. "He's my friend!"

"Oh, I—I don't know." Mal held his head in confusion. "I—I'm sorry. I didn't mean to . . ."

Regina helped the surprised Joey get up from the ground.

"Joey, this is Mal," Regina said with a sigh. "He's new here. And he doesn't remember anything."

"Nothing?" Joey swept the dirt from his pants as he kept eyeing Mal. "He doesn't know who he is and stuff?"

"Yeah." Regina shot a wary smile toward Mal, who just stood there like a lost puppy.

"Mal, this is my friend, Joey," said Regina. "Joey, this is Mal. He just wandered into my hut in the middle of the night, because he thought he knew me."

"But you don't?" Joey reached out and shook hands with Mal. "Know each other?"

"No, we don't," said Regina, but she had a feeling Mal still wouldn't agree with her on that.

Mal kept looking at Joey with suspicious eyes, like he was waiting for Joey to do something bad.

Joey didn't linger on Mal's face for long. Regina wasn't even sure if he had even noticed Mal's unusual features.

"So, you don't remember anything, huh?" Joey slid his hands into his pockets. "I'm sure some memories will come back to you here. Things have a tendency to come to light here in Andara."

Mal nodded with tight lips, his gaze still filled with distrust.

"So what was that about earlier?" Joey pointed behind himself, like it was possible to point back at the past.

"I don't know," Mal said, shaking his head. "I thought you were going to hurt her."

Joey nodded, brows furrowed. "Why, exactly?"

"I'm not sure, it was like an instinct, all right? I'm sorry." Mal's voice was more annoyed than regretful.

"Okay, umm," said Joey, turning away from Mal and dropping the topic like hot coal, "want to go for a walk, Regina? Maybe check on Snow and Pyro? You can come too, Mal, if you want."

"Sure, let's go." Regina nodded. "Snow is great, you'll like her, Mal. Pyro's . . . okay too."

Brunorth trotting behind them, they started toward the ocean, since that was where Snow and Pyro often sat.

"Pyro's okay too?" Joey asked Regina with a smirk.

"He's not so bad," Regina said with a smile.

Regina still couldn't talk about Pyro without thinking about Jasper. She hadn't told anyone about the night she had seen Jasper on the edge of the woods. They had stared at each other in grieving silence, then Jasper turned around and left without a word, returning to Mount Napharata. There was almost no trace of their friendship left. But Regina still hadn't lost hope. It wasn't impossible for Jasper to return to the Field of Cetana like nothing had happened. Unlikely, maybe, but not impossible.

Regina and Joey walked in front and Mal followed them. For a couple of minutes, at least. Then Mal forced himself between Regina and Joey without a word.

Regina and Joey glanced at each other, but they didn't say anything. Even if Regina wanted to say something, Agnitio's warning would have made her swallow her words.

They reached the beach in silence. On the sparkling sand, Snow and Pyro sat. Their blond heads were almost blinding in the sunlight. A plate of food lay between them.

"Hi, guys," said Regina as they walked up to them.

"Oh, hi." Snow turned back to look at them.

"Hey." Pyro did the same as he shielded his blue eyes from the rising sun. When he saw Mal, a sound escaped from his lips that was most likely a stifled shriek kind of thing. "Who's your friend?"

"This is Mal," said Regina. "He's new here. He has no memories."

"Oh, you have amnesia?" said Snow. "Poor thing." Similar to Joey, she also seemed unaffected by the sight of Mal.

Regina started feeling increasingly bad for screaming when Mal had woken her up. Another thing she had in common only with Pyro besides the Dark Oracle. *Great.*

"So, you're starting your journey today? Or tomorrow?" Snow asked Mal and tapped the ground, gesturing him to sit down next to her.

Mal sat down in the sand, but not at all where Snow had tapped the ground, but a lot farther from her. Snow didn't seem to mind.

"I think I'm starting today. Not much is keeping me here, you know." Mal glanced at Regina. "I just want to get it over with."

"I get it." Snow nodded. "I'm sure you'll get a lot of answers here. We all have."

"You are all done with the journey?" Mal asked.

They all nodded.

"We're just guarding the balance now for a little while," said Snow.

"Balance? What balance?"

"I guess you'll find out soon." Snow scratched her head and smiled.

Mal sighed like he was already sick of everything.

"So, Regina," Snow said, turning around. She reached for Regina's leg, but before she could touch her, Mal landed between them with a karate chop, slicing Snow's hand away.

In that moment, there it was again—the flickering apparition: the dog-like black skeleton right next to Mal, appearing and then disappearing as fast as it had come.

"Ouch!" Snow massaged her aching hand and shot an angry glance toward Mal. "What's the deal, Mal?"

Regina was not sure if anyone else saw what she had.

Mal plopped back on the ground and covered his mouth with his hand. "I'm sorry, I don't know," he mumbled.

"Did you just hit Snow?" Pyro got up from the ground.

"Pyro, calm down." Regina stood up as well.

Pyro looked like something was boiling behind his face, ready to explode. "I don't care who or *what* you are, you can't act like that around here."

"Pyro." Regina now stood in front of Pyro, a couple inches from his face. Even so, it still took the blond boy a few moments to tear his raging eyes from Mal.

"We have to watch how we act around him," Regina said as quietly as she could. "Agnitio warned me. Lives are at stake, Pyro. Calm down."

"Yeah, because he's a maniac," said Pyro, whispering back with anger.

Regina made a face that emphasized what she had said. "Just trust me and calm down. Have a little compassion, geez."

"It's okay, I'm going." Mal had stood up too, ready to leave. "Regina, will you come with me?"

Regina turned and looked at Mal with surprise. "Me? No, Mal, I already completed my journey."

"Okay, then . . . could you, at least, come with me until the forest or something?"

Regina glanced at Joey, Snow and Pyro. From the three of them, only Pyro showed what he felt with eyebrows raised high and mouth spread wide.

But Agnitio's words kept bothering Regina like a nagging child.

"Sure, I'll go," she said finally, making herself forget about the boy's strangeness and his black skeleton dog.

"And she never came back," whispered Pyro, but Snow shoved him with her elbow.

Regina smiled at Mal, but inside, she desperately hoped Pyro was not right.

4 CHILD OF LOSTHAN

"I think it would be a good idea to take a nap, at least, before you leave," Regina said to Mal. "Who knows when you'll get to sleep next." She could only imagine how tired Mal must have been without any sleep. She also wanted to win a little time before she ventured into the forest with him.

"You're right, I'll lie down a little before I set off." Mal's expression was tense, like he was fed up with everything already. He turned away and began walking away. "It was nice meeting you guys," he said, not even turning back to face them.

Regina looked at Snow and Pyro, and they looked back at her with raised eyebrows. Regina shrugged and went after Mal.

"It was nice knowing you, Regina," Pyro whispered after her, to which she shot an angry look back at him.

Joey walked next to Regina with his hands in his pockets. Unlike Pyro, he didn't seem annoyed with Mal.

"So, what's going to happen now?" Mal waited for Regina to catch up to him.

"Well, I'm guessing you'll slowly start to remember. Agnitio must have had a reason to bring you here right when you lost your memories."

Brunorth walked next to them peacefully. Regina wondered why the dragon was so friendly with Mal even though the boy seemed to have those violent tendencies. Maybe he had calmed down during his rebirth.

"Everything will only get better." Regina smiled. "I'm sure of it."

Mal glanced at Regina and his face softened as he did. The weight of the world lifted off him when he looked at her.

"Wait, Mal!" Snow ran after them, Pyro following her. "Take this," she said when she caught up to them.

"What's this?" Mal accepted the shining object from Snow's hand.

"It's a crystal I got from a very special place here in Andara," Snow said with a smile. "I hope it will help you on your journey."

"Yeah, dude"—Pyro scratched his head and looked at the ground—"I mean, my journey wasn't the easiest either, but, umm . . . it must be extra hard without any memories and all." He looked at Mal and bit on his lip. "But you can do it, you know? Just . . . keep going." He nodded, emphasizing what he had said. "And, uh, sorry about back there." He gestured back toward the beach where they had been sitting.

Mal looked at the shining piece of crystal in his hand. He smiled a strange smile as if he couldn't fully understand what was happening. "Thanks," he said, looking up at them. His face was not hard anymore. Not at all. "I'm sorry too. I hope I get some answers here. To all of this." He shook his head. "I hope I'm not as scary as I feel inside sometimes."

"I'm sure you're not." Snow placed her hand on Mal's shoulder for a long moment, and Regina could see the boy grow tense under her touch. "You'll do great. And when you get back, we can have tea or something. I make the best Andarian salads." She smiled.

"Thanks." Mal didn't look at Snow; he either stared at the crystal in his hand or the ground in front of him. "I'll go get some rest before I leave." He gestured toward the huts then turned around to leave. "Thanks again," he said, and he turned back to do so this time.

"Find us when you come back," said Pyro.

Walking away from them, Mal nodded.

"What happened, guys?" Regina asked Pyro and Snow with a smile.

"I don't know," said Pyro with a shrug and turned

around, walking back to the beach from where they had come.

"You said lives were at stake," said Snow. "It never hurts to be nice."

"Was that crystal," said Regina, "from the Island of Pyara?

Snow nodded. "Astraea let me keep it."

"That's very nice of you. To give it to Mal," said Regina.

Snow shrugged. "It's not like I can take it back home. At least, I don't think so. Well, I think it will be of better use with him, anyway."

"You're the best, Snow." Regina gave her friend a nice and tight hug.

Snow laughed. "Go, get some rest. You look a little tired."

"You are my ancient friend for a reason," said Regina and waved bye to Snow as they set off in opposite directions—Regina toward her hut, and Snow toward Pyro.

"What a change of heart," said Joey.

"I'm glad they did that." Regina smiled. "I think Mal really needs it."

"I hope he really will make it back here."

"I hope so too," said Regina, resting her gaze on Mal.

"Did you notice the Corruptor too?" Joey asked, out of the blue.

"The what?" Regina looked at him.

Joey turned toward her and looked at her in silence for a moment. "The Corruptor. Haven't you heard about them? There's an old folktale that says they're the demons who guide the residents of Losthan." Joey took a piece of paper and a pencil out from his pocket.

Regina's breath froze inside her throat. She remembered learning about Losthan in school. Losthan, the town that stood alone, lay between borders, not having a country of its own. Losthan had its own rules, and they were not ones of equality, peace or freedom. The children of Losthan were oppressed, growing up among violence, without a chance of ever leaving. The rest of the world often thought of them as the most ruthless group of uncivilized brutes.

Joey scribbled something on the paper and handed it to Regina. "According to the folktale, this is what a Corruptor looks like."

Regina started biting her lower lip as she stared at Joey's drawing. It was a black skeleton of a dog, encompassed by smoke. Regina swallowed.

"I saw it," she said, her throat dry.

Joey slid the drawing in his pocket. "Yeah, I saw it too." He looked after Mal.

"I'll come get you," Mal yelled back to Regina. "When I wake up, okay?"

Regina couldn't reply immediately. She just stared at the boy for a long moment. "Okay!" she made herself say.

When Mal disappeared inside his hut, Regina turned to Joey. "What does this mean?"

Joey shrugged. "It means he's from Losthan. And that folktales are truer than one might think."

"That's why he's so weird," Regina said, mostly to herself.

"Don't think too much about it. You should get some rest."

"You don't think we should be concerned?" asked Regina.

"No. I don't think we should be concerned," Joey answered like it was the most natural thing in the world.

"Okay." Regina let her tension subside. "I will go get some rest. I'm really tired."

Joey smiled his nonchalant half-smile and started toward his own hut.

Once in her hut, Regina lay down on her bed, exhausted. It might have been the first time she felt this tired in Andara. She didn't want to think about the strange boy or Losthan or anything. She just wanted to rest.

Brunorth curled up next to her, and it didn't take long for both of them to fall asleep.

Regina was walking on an underground pathway. A pathway that felt strangely familiar. Roots of trees dangled above her head like octopus arms. Whispers disturbed the silence.

Placing one foot in front of the other, Regina walked through the narrow tunnel. The whispers grew louder as she got closer to their source. They sounded like kids gossiping, laughing, telling secrets in their hiding spot.

Regina wanted to know those secrets. So she quickened her steps.

The tunnel took a sudden turn, so she did too. And she was faced with them. A bunch of kids stood at the end of the tunnel. They wore rags for clothes. Their hair was unkempt. But that was not what made Regina's feet root into the ground. All of them—each and every one—had a skull right on top of their heads—wolf skulls.

They all stopped talking and stared at Regina. Their eyes were vicious as they looked Regina up and down.

"You," one of the kids said, taking a step toward Regina. "You think you're so clever. With your big heart and whatnot."

Another child shook his head. "You should be careful who you choose to be kind with."

"Not everybody deserves it, you know," said another.

"Would you be that kind to us?" asked the fourth.

Regina couldn't take her eyes off of them. There were so many. Boys, girls, some older, some younger than her.

She nodded, answering the boy's question.

"Not many people were kind to us, you know," said a girl. "While we were alive."

"Us kids only have each other."

"You wouldn't want to be friends with the one who hurt us, would you?" asked a little girl.

"The one who sent us here."

"The one who made us disappear."

"Because he was mad."

"You saw how mad he gets."

"Over the littlest things."

"The littlest things."

"It was the freak."

"The freak did it."

"He's crazy."

Regina took a couple steps back. "What are you talking about? I—I don't understand."

A boy with curly brown hair tilted his head to the side and said, "You, little miss, with your kindness and big heart, have just made friends with a very-very bad person."

"Do you mean . . . Mal?"

At the mention of his name, all the kids hissed like cats trying to scare an enemy away.

"Yes, miss," the curly-haired boy said. "We are all dead, because Mal killed us all."

5. UPSETTING PRESENCE

Regina woke up in a cold sweat. She sat up on her bed. Her breaths didn't come easy.

Mal . . . is . . . a murderer. Thoughts rushed around in her mind, and they made her stomach tight.

Brunorth gently poked her with his snout, letting her know he was there.

Who were all those kids? Were they all Fyes? They didn't seem regretful about their lives. And they didn't seem to want to help her either. Or was this a warning?

Regina wiped the sweat off her forehead. *Mal forgot he killed a bunch of people.*

Regina wished she could dismiss what she had heard in her dream, she wished she could forget it and think it was only a dream and nothing more. But she couldn't. Mal's weird behavior, his violent outbursts, the Corruptor next to him—it all made sense.

But what does he want . . . with me?

Regina didn't want to rest anymore. She jumped out of bed and looked back at the sheets like ants were crawling all over them. She definitely didn't want to go back to sleep.

She rushed out of her hut, Brunorth right behind her. She didn't stop until she reached Joey's.

"Joey!" She knocked on his door. "Are you here?"

"What's wrong, Regina?" Joey opened the door. There he stood, with pieces of his black hair fallen over his face and his warm brown eyes sparkling with worry.

The tension inside Regina disintegrated. The dream she had seen became just that—a bad dream.

"I just . . . had a nightmare," she said.

"In the five minutes you were asleep? That's an accomplishment. Come on in."

"Do you think he killed all those kids?" Regina asked after telling Joey about her dream.

They sat at the circular wooden table and ate little slices of an apple sort of fruit from a bowl that looked more like a cauldron than anything.

"I have no idea." Joey shook his head and placed a slice of fruit in his mouth. "But I know someone who might know."

"Who? Agnitio?"

"Yeah, but no. We should ask someone who could interpret your dream for sure. The one who knows a lot about Fyes and souls and such."

"Y'sis." Regina nodded. "She has to know who those kids in my dream were. They are probably with her right now. As orbs, I mean." She was already standing up from the table, ready to go.

Joey stuffed a couple of slices of fruit in his mouth and pushed the rest of the bowl to Regina, who ate the remaining two pieces, then they were off.

They were on their way toward Dara Forest when someone shouted after them.

"Regina! I'm ready to go. You coming?"

"Oh, right." Regina made a face like there was something sour in her mouth. "I forgot about Mal. I'm supposed to go with him."

"He didn't get a lot of sleep either," said Joey.

They stood in place as Mal walked to them.

"You weren't going to leave me here, were you?" Mal asked with a smile, but Regina couldn't even look at him.

"No, of course not. I just thought you were still sleeping."

"I couldn't sleep. I'd rather be moving instead. Not knowing anything is killing me."

"Mm." Regina nodded, turning away from Mal.

"What's wrong, little one? You're acting very odd." Mal put his hand on Regina's shoulder.

Regina immediately jumped away.

Mal's hand hung in the air where she had left it. He stood in silence for a long moment. "It's my face, isn't it?" He let his hand down. "I disgust you."

"No!" Regina said, almost shouting. She looked at Mal now. "Of course not. It's just . . . I had a bad dream, that's all."

"She did that to me, too, don't worry." Joey waved his hand, signaling it was not a big deal.

Mal looked at him with suspicion, but nodded anyway.

"Let's go," said Regina, trying to smile at Mal. "Your journey awaits."

"Oh, such a lucky one you are," said a familiar raspy

voice once they stepped into the woods.

"Who said that?" Mal looked around with caution.

"It's probably Lagurus," said Regina. "Yes, there he is." She pointed at the large tree with cracks in its bark that looked like a face. "He's a tree."

"A talking tree?" Mal stared at Lagurus, wide-eyed.

The old tree laughed. "My boy, you are fortunate, to have forgotten who you were."

"Do you know who I am? Can you tell me?"

"Oh, my dear boy, that is not the question you should be asking. A chance like this doesn't come around often. To forget who you are."

"What should I be asking then?"

"You should ask yourself who you want to be. Because right now, you can be anyone."

"That's what Agnitio said as well," said Regina.

"Yes, well, if Agnitio has already told you, there's no need for me to tire my mouth." Lagurus sounded kind of hurt, and in the next moment, the cracks that were his face disappeared and only the ordinary bark of a tree remained.

"Did I just," said Regina, "insult him? I didn't mean to."

"Trees might be more sensitive than people, maybe."

Mal shrugged. "Let's just go."

They kept walking through the forest. Since Regina and Joey wanted to talk to Y'sis anyway, they thought they could go with Mal until they found her.

"If you see lights in every color of the rainbow, tell me," said Regina. "Because that's probably Y'sis."

"Or if you hear a song as gentle as a whisper," added Joey. "That's probably her too."

"So, why do you want to talk to this girl?" asked Mal.

"You know, it's just . . . we're friends." Regina looked around, trying hard to locate the colorful orbs. "You know, Mal," she said after not finding anything that could be Y'sis, "I think you really should just go through Andara without trying to find out who you were. I would take Agnitio's advice. And Lagurus'. Not that it's any of my business. But I think who you want to be is more important than the person you were up until now."

> *Little sparkles, don't you fear*
> *All is done, the end's not near*
> *The forest's waiting for your cheer*
> *I am here for you, my dear.*

"Y'sis!" Regina exclaimed.

"It's coming from there." Joey pointed at an unusual gathering of trees.

Now that they looked more closely, the rainbow of colors mystically seeped through the leaves.

All three of them started toward the lights. Regina thought that Mal would depart after a while, and she and Joey would stay and talk to Y'sis.

They stepped through the trees, and there Y'sis sat, on a branch above all of them. As usual, the orbs danced around her joyfully. Until Regina, Joey and Mal walked closer to them.

Once they got near, their colorful dance stopped. Regina felt like they were looking at them. Like someone unwanted had wondered into their domain.

"Hi, Y'si—" Regina couldn't finish her greeting.

The orbs started toward them like a little army charging toward the enemy.

"What in the skies are you doing?" Y'sis' voice was still like a soothing song. Regina still didn't understand how she could see from behind all her messy white hair that was so long, it dangled below her legs.

The orbs flew straight into Mal's face like colorful bugs

ready to bite the life out of him.

"Uh, go away!" Mal tried to chase them away with his arms to no avail. "This feels weird!"

"Come back here, right now." Y'sis snapped her fingers, to which every orb froze in the air. They hovered for a moment then flew back to Y'sis. "You have to behave yourselves." Y'sis' feet swung happily from the branch she was sitting on. "Regina, Joey, how nice to see you. Mal, so nice to meet you. Welcome to Dara Forest."

Mal waved awkwardly, not knowing what to think of the situation.

"Unfortunately, I have to ask you to continue onward. This doesn't happen often, but your presence is upsetting these souls, and their serenity is vital at this stage. Please, as a token of my apology, take this flower. I hope it will guide you when you most need it."

"Umm, thanks," said Mal, but he didn't know what she was thinking, since Y'sis hadn't given him anything.

"Open your palm," said Y'sis.

Mal did as he was told, and in his palm, a small white flower rested.

"Oh, thanks." Mal smiled and seemed just a tiny bit

touched. Even though he didn't remember anything, he mustn't have gotten many gifts in his forgotten life.

He looked at Regina, and the joy she saw on his face made her forget everything she had been told about him. The genuine happiness on it was as pure as sunlight. All from a simple little flower.

"Come, look," Mal said to Regina, "you love flowers."

Regina looked at him with the mixture of sadness and worry.

"Oh, yes, sorry." Mal waved his arms around like he was trying to chase something away. Much like he had done with the attacking orbs. "We don't know each other."

"I'll get going now," he said, turning away. "Thank you Y'sis. Very much." He looked at Y'sis as he spoke.

"You are most welcome, Mal," said Y'sis. "Don't forget all the advice you've gotten. And when in doubt, look at the stars."

Mal nodded. Just when he was about to disappear between the trees, he turned back toward Regina but continued walking backward.

"I'll come back for you," he said, right before the darkness of the forest swallowed him whole.

6 SKULL-CARRIERS

Regina looked at the empty shadow where Mal had disappeared. She kept swirling and turning his last words in her mind. All the movement inside her head made her stomach feel small.

"Regina?" Joey's voice sounded like a distant echo in Regina's ear.

"Yes?" Regina turned toward him with raised brows and wide open eyes.

"Aren't you asking Y'sis your question?"

"My question?" All the worrying thoughts had pushed everything else out of her mind, so she had a hard time remembering what Joey was referring to. "Oh, my question, yes."

Regina lifted her eyes to Y'sis. She sat on the branch

with her head moving left and right like she was listening to a song only she could hear. The colorful orbs around her floated peacefully. Except for one. An orb that had a pinkish, purplish color escaped from the group like a fugitive. It flew in the exact direction Mal had left.

"A-a!" Y'sis sang and snapped her fingers. The orb froze just before it could disappear between the trees. "You know that's not allowed. I truly hate to be a cold-hearted faun, but it's best if you stay for now. I will allow it later. That's a promise."

The orb glided back to Y'sis dutifully. It was not easy, maybe not even possible, to tell an orb's emotions, but Regina could have sworn that this one was sad.

"I had a dream, Y'sis," Regina said when the orb arrived next to Y'sis, "and I was hoping you could help me make sense of it."

"Dreams can cause a lot of havoc, can't they?" Y'sis mused. "Even when they mean nothing most of the time." She looked at Regina from under her messy blanket of hair. "But here in Andara, they do mean something more often than not."

"So what does it mean if, like, dozens of Fyes appear in my dream?"

"Dozens of Fyes?" Y'sis pushed her bottom lip with her finger. "Goodness. That's simply not possible." She looked up at the tree's green leaves hanging above her. "Unless . . ."

Regina waited a long moment, but Y'sis didn't continue.

"Unless?" Regina said.

Y'sis looked at her again. Her purple eyes were clear under her hair. "Unless they were not Fyes."

"But they all had skulls on their heads."

"All Fyes have skulls on their heads. But not all those

who have skulls on their heads are Fyes."

Regina's brows furrowed just a little.

"The skull on the head simply signifies death. Nothing less, nothing more. It means its carrier has lost its shell in the normal world. That's why we call them skull-carriers."

Regina lifted her hand to her chin. "So those were . . . just a bunch of dead people?"

"If you were in the normal world, I would say it was just a dream. A dream is usually just a dream in the normal world. But since you're in Andara . . ." She gazed at the orbs dancing around her. "Yes," she said with a sigh. "Those were dead people in your dream."

"Oh, wow." Regina let her hand fall next to her. Actual people had spoken to her in her dream, there was no doubt about that now. "Do skull-carriers . . . tell the truth?" Regina was afraid of the answer.

"Well"—Y'sis sat on her hands—"skull-carriers are just people, you see. And people don't always tell the truth."

"So they were lying," Regina mumbled under her breath.

"No," said Y'sis in her song-like voice, playfully shaking her head. "No, they weren't lying."

Regina and Y'sis looked at each other for a long

moment. Y'sis knew what the skull-carriers had told Regina. And she also knew they were telling the truth.

"Fyes are special kind of skull-carriers. They are wise and see everything as it truly is. They have transcended their worldly limitations. But all other skull-carriers—they usually stay . . . how should I put it"—Y'sis shielded her mouth from the orbs and lowered her voice to a whisper—"as stupid as they were as humans." She straightened up and smiled. "They were upset just now for the same reason they were upset in their lives. And in your dream." Y'sis gestured toward the orbs.

Regina's eyes widened as she slowly pointed at the orbs with a weak finger. "These souls . . . were the ones in my dream?"

Y'sis nodded.

"So that's why they attacked Mal," Joey said to himself.

"You should get going now." Y'sis stood up on the branch. The orbs around her moved as she moved. "My job is to calm disturbed souls. And these little ones have a lot of calming to do." She hopped onto a branch on the next tree.

"Thanks, Y'sis," said Regina, "for telling us all this."

"You're welcome," said Y'sis, hopping onto another

branch again. "There is just one more thing I think I should add." She straightened up and looked at them. "The truth—it changes in every human's eye. Just because someone isn't lying, doesn't mean they are telling the truth." With that, she hopped onto the next tree and out of Regina's sight.

"What does that mean?" Regina asked Joey.

"That what the skull-carriers told you wasn't necessarily the truth?" said Joey with a shrug.

"They just didn't know they were lying." Regina lifted her hand to her chin.

"How can someone not know when they are lying?" asked Joey.

"Well, they don't *know* they are not telling the truth, so they are not lying exactly . . ."

"They just don't know the truth themselves."

"But they think they do, yes." Regina nodded but after a long pause, she said, "I'm still confused. Is Mal a killer or not?"

Joey looked at her for a short while, his eyes jumping left and right on hers, then shrugged, his nose wrinkled. "He might be, he might not be."

"Well, that didn't get us any further," said Regina and

turned around so they could go back to the field.

But something made her stop in her steps. Someone was watching her from the shadows of the trees. She saw the dark silhouette, but nothing else.

Regina swallowed. Mal must have stayed to eavesdrop on them. And now he knew what they knew about him.

"What's up?" asked Joey, stepping next to her.

"Nothing, nothing." Regina didn't want to trouble Joey, so she started walking the other way, away from the dark silhouette.

Brunorth didn't question her choice, he walked right beside her.

"The field's this way," said Joey, pointing toward the silhouette.

"I know, I just thought we could take a little detour." Regina didn't even stop to talk.

"Okay," said Joey with a shrug and followed her.

Regina walked through tall grass and several bushes, her pace faster than it should have been if she wanted to seem calm. She glanced back from time to time, checking if the silhouette was following them or not. She didn't see it anymore.

"What's wrong, Regina? What are you looking at?" Joey looked back every time Regina did, but he couldn't see anything either.

"Nothing, I just heard a noise. Maybe it's a cute Andarian animal or something. Wouldn't want to miss that," said Regina wiggling through a particularly spiky bush.

When they stepped out from the thorny branches, a familiar building towered over them. No matter how many times Regina saw the dark castle, it never ceased to make her uncomfortable.

7 AMONG THE MADMAN'S COLLECTION

As Regina rested her eyes on the tall castle piercing through the trees, an idea came to her mind.

"Joey, we should go in," she said, turning toward the boy.

"To Eris' castle? Why?"

"Do you remember that madman room? The one filled with newspaper articles?"

Joey swept a piece of black hair from his eyes. "How could I forget?" he said the question more as a statement. "The article about me was in there too." He looked up at the tower like the memory was heavy for him to carry.

"Yeah, but that's all sorted now." Regina smiled and placed her hand on Joey's shoulder. "Don't be sad about something that's already done. You're a Nayaka after all.

You have one of the rarest souls in the world."

Joey looked at her, half of his lip turned upward. "Why do you want to go up there?" he asked in a soft voice.

"Because there might be something about Mal in that room." Regina let her hand fall down and looked up at the castle. "There are a bunch of articles up there, and all of them are about violent crimes. If Mal is really a killer, there's a fat chance there will be something about him too." She shrugged as she looked at Joey. "It's worth a shot, no?"

"Why not," said Joey, and they made their way to the castle together.

"Don't look at the wall," said Regina when they reached the stairs leading up to the large entrance. She didn't want to see the hostile old lady that always looked back at her, almost as her reflection. She may or may not have been Regina's future self, and she just didn't want to deal with her right now.

She buried her face into Joey's shoulder. She only realized what she was doing when they reached the top of the stairs. Her face was burning hot as she pulled it away slowly, trying to act like nothing out of the ordinary had happened.

Joey didn't say anything. He was looking at the large black door in front of them. Maybe he didn't even notice.

Regina exhaled a deep breath and tucked her hair behind her ear. HOSTIS HUMANI GENERIS—the words carved into the wood of the door still held the memory of the one who had lived here. The once-human who liked to think of himself as the enemy of the human race. Regina was glad he had been banished to the Living Dead, the people who chose to stay in Andara forever, thus throwing away their lives. Eris had done enough damage. Regina still comforted herself with the belief that without him, Jasper might not have attacked Pyro.

The large door in front of them was slightly open, so they slid inside. Dragontears had grown all over the encyclopedias that were stuffed inside the room from floor to ceiling.

Regina and Joey made their way to the other side of the room and all the way up to the top of the tower—the madman room, as Regina had called it. The hole in the right wall of the room allowed light to illuminate the space. In the daylight, it didn't look as much like the hideout of a madman. It was just an exceptionally old room with a lot of even older newspaper cutouts plastered all over the walls.

But not even the daylight could make what lay on the pages easier to read.

"Uh, so if we want to find an article about Mal, we have to look through"—she swallowed and looked around the room with narrow eyes—"a lot of other horrible stories."

Regina hadn't been comfortable when they were in this room the first time. She couldn't look at the articles and wanted to be anywhere else but there. The unpleasant experience hadn't come to her mind when she had come up with the idea of climbing up here again.

"I'll look through them if you don't want to," said Joey, already looking at the yellowed pieces of paper on one of the walls. "This way I can hide any other articles about me too." He looked back at Regina with a playful smile.

Regina rolled her eyes at him, but her mouth told she was not annoyed at all.

"I'll be fine," she said, turning toward another wall. She already monitored her breathing, keeping it calm and deep, the exhales always longer then the inhales. She wanted to lower her chances of freaking out as much as possible.

But she didn't even get the chance to read one article,

and her breath was already stuck in her throat.

She looked at the picture without blinking, not being able to say anything for a long moment. She might have even forgotten to breathe.

"Well, Joey, jokes on you," she said finally, still not able to look away from the article in front of her.

"What did you find?" asked Joey, the tone of his voice

revealing he sensed Regina's tension.

"I didn't find an article about you," said Regina. "But I found one about me."

8. THE GIRL WITH LOVE IN HER EYES

"That does look exactly like you," said Joey, astounded. "Is it? Is it you?" He took a closer look at the yellowed piece of paper. "The words are so faded. Is it that old?"

"The sun was shining on it." Regina pointed at the hole on the wall next to them. "It must have faded the letters. The date's readable under the article. Look. It was written a year ago."

"Wow, yeah, I see. So . . . *is* this you?" Joey looked at Regina with raised brows.

Regina shook her head. "I've never seen those clothes before. The ones she's wearing. It's not me."

Joey looked back at the picture, and so did Regina. The girl with light brown hair and a loving smile looked just like Regina. Even the way she rested her hands in her lap,

68

shoulders raised, a little tense, was a pose Regina could see herself sitting in, often.

The girl wasn't looking at them. That loving smile was not meant for the camera, but for the person behind it. A smile like that couldn't be wasted for a lens.

Her eyes sparkled with something that could only be described as adoration for the person they rested on.

She didn't care about her old and oversized clothes—someone who smiled like that couldn't have cared.

"I don't think I ever looked at anyone like that," said Regina.

"I don't think I've ever seen anyone look at anyone like that," said Joey.

Regina reached for the article and pulled it off the wall. Only rotting bricks lay behind it.

"Some words are clearer than others," she said, trying to make out at least something from the text that surrounded the picture. "*Dead*, for example, look."

"Yep, that's definitely a *dead*."

"*Killer*. Isn't this a *killer*?"

Joey nodded. "I think it is."

"And this, right here, what is this?"

Joey swallowed.

"So you see what I see."

"I think I do."

"*Mal.*"

"Yep."

"Is this serious?" Regina looked at Joey like the article had offended her. "*Dead, killer, Mal?*" She raised her eyebrows and shook her head. "This is insane, Joey, insane."

"Let's not jump to conclusions, it's just three words." Joey tried to ease the tension.

"This is too much of a coincidence, Joey." Regina had forgotten about monitoring her breathing and was already swallowing huge gasps, not letting much of it back out. "What if Mal really did do something to this girl, and that's why he's been acting so weird with me? Because the impulse or whatever that made him hurt her is still there? And he thinks, or *feels*, I'm her?"

Joey looked at her with sympathetic eyes and shook his head slowly. Not in a "what you're saying doesn't make sense" way, but more in a "I really don't know what to say" way.

"I'm going to try to read this somehow." Regina stuffed

the article in her pocket. "Jasper could probably tell me how I could bring the words back. I'm sure we can recover at least a couple more. Maybe the article is not even about what we think it is about. I hope it's not."

"It's just three words," said Joey. "It can be anything. But the girl in the picture is the person Mal knew. Not you. At least we know that much."

"Yeah, it was worth coming up here, at least. I'm glad. Now let's get out of here."

"I found something as well." Joey held up a newspaper cutout—one that was much smaller than the one Regina had found.

"Really?" Regina looked at the paper. It only had one sentence on it and a date.

NEXT PRINCE OF LOSTHAN FOUND

Regina raised her eyebrows. "What's this?" She flipped the piece of paper around to see if there was something else on the back, but there wasn't. "This is an article?"

"Look at the date," said Joey. "It's brand new."

"It's even from after we came to Andara." Regina looked

at Joey. "This must have been one of the last pieces Eris put up here."

"If the walls don't update themselves somehow on their own, yeah."

"The Prince of Losthan," Regina thought aloud, looking at the cutout. "The prince is who governs the town, right? And they appoint him with all sorts of shady methods."

"Like burning down buildings and appointing the only survivor, yeah." Joey nodded with a sigh.

"That's not very civilized," said Regina.

"Losthan's not very civilized."

"Okay, well . . ." A chill ran down Regina's spine. "Let's get out of here for real. This place is giving me the creeps."

They exited the black castle and left it behind as they walked back toward the Field of Cetana. Brunorth seemed to be bored and didn't show much interest in what they were doing.

Joey threw the idea around that Mal was probably not a killer, and all of this was just a huge misunderstanding. He even mentioned that they would laugh about it in the end. At that moment, Regina couldn't imagine laughing about any of it, but hoped that Joey was right.

A rustle behind them broke into their discussion. Brunorth jerked his head up. Regina turned around, and saw the dark silhouette again, watching them.

"I think someone's watching us," she whispered to Joey. "By the bushes."

Another rustle. Brunorth ran toward the sound, and when Joey turned and saw the figure, he ran after the dragon as well.

The silhouette disappeared as fast as it had appeared, running away with a loud rustle of leaves.

Joey stopped when he realized there was no way to reach the figure, and Brunorth did too, growling after the perpetrator.

"Who do you think it was?" asked Regina when Joey came back to her.

"I think it was a person. A human, I mean."

"He was watching us when we were talking to Y'sis."

"What? Really? Why didn't you say something?"

Regina shrugged. "I just didn't want to worry you."

"Do you think it's Mal?"

"Who else could it be?" said Regina, disillusioned. She had already had enough of this day.

"But didn't Agnitio say we should be nice to him or something?" asked Joey. "Why would he do that if Mal was a killer and wanted to hurt you?"

"I'm not sure. Because we should be nice to everyone? Pff, I don't know."

"I guess we'll find out soon enough."

They walked out of the forest and to Regina's hut. The sun was already starting to set.

Regina and Joey ate and drank in her hut and tried to make the words appear on the faded newspaper cutout with all sorts of ideas like raising it toward the light or even giving it to a Nangrass. They managed to rip it out of its little hands before it sleepily began eating the paper. The screaming that followed didn't quiet down for a long while.

After they didn't manage to recover a single word besides *killer*, *dead* and *Mal*, Joey left to retire to his hut, and Regina also got ready for bed. It had been a long day.

She placed the article under her pillow, hoping that the words would magically appear by morning. She was in Andara, after all, anything could happen.

Brunorth curled up next to her on the bed. Regina pushed her face into the dragon's back. His scales were not as hard as they looked. At least not when Regina touched them.

Maybe the dragon's warm breath would make the words reappear. Maybe the night. Or the light of the stars in the dark. But neither of those did.

Calm sleep didn't come either. Strange figures were watching Regina while awake, but even stranger figures were waiting for her in the land of dreams.

Killer, dead, Mal. Killer, dead, Mal. Killer, dead, Mal. Regina walked under the roots again, on the underground pathway. *Killer, dead, Mal.* The three words echoed on the walls like forbidden whispers.

The path kept twisting in front of Regina. She didn't know what was waiting for her at the end this time.

She turned a sharp corner. A girl was crouching on the path. She was drawing something on the dusty ground. The skull on top of her head was pearly white.

"Killer, dead, Mal." The girl repeated the words without standing up or even looking at Regina. "You don't have much to go on, huh?" Regina couldn't decide if her voice was hostile or simply indifferent.

Regina had stopped when she saw the girl. She kept

looking at her, but she couldn't see her face. Locks of brown hair covered it as she kept drawing with her fingers in the dust.

"What—what are you drawing?" Regina took a step closer.

"You wouldn't understand," said the girl.

"What's there to understand? Isn't it just a drawing?" Regina's voice was as kind as she could make it. She took another step toward the girl, who turned and looked at her like an angry animal trying to scare an intruder away. Only the snarl was missing from her face, but everything else was in her eyes.

Regina took a step back and held her hands up defensively. But she couldn't stop her jaw from dropping when she saw the girl's face. It was almost like looking into a mirror—a very unfriendly one.

The girl's hair was a couple shades darker than Regina's ash brown, and her skin was warm beige instead of Regina's pale ivory.

The girl stood up and trod to Regina. She stopped right in front of her and slowly looked Regina up and down. She then pursed her lips, narrowed her eyes and stomped back to where she had come from, continuing to fiddle in the dust with her finger.

"She's not like me at all," she mumbled to herself, sulking. "I don't know why you think she's like me. Idiot. She's not like me at all. Not in the slightest."

"Are you talking about Mal? *To* Mal?" said Regina. "You know him, right? *Knew* him. I mean know him." She was desperately trying not to offend the girl, but she had no idea what was or was not appropriate to say to the deceased.

"I *know* him." The girl stood up, looking into Regina's green eyes with her identical ones. "I will always *know* him, and I will always be by his side." She walked up to Regina and pushed her finger into her chest. "So you better get off his back." Her eyes were narrowed. "You're not the one he loves." She lowered her finger. "He just doesn't know it yet." She shot another sharp look at Regina. "*Yet.*" She turned her back on Regina and started walking away. "He'll remember."

"But," said Regina, and the girl stopped in her steps, "you can't go back." Regina didn't know what made her say the words. They just slipped out. The girl might not have known that she was utterly and irreversibly dead. And Regina telling her would not make her like her more.

The girl stood frozen for a long moment. Then she turned around and looked at Regina. Her eyes were filled to the brim with tears. Her lips trembled as she pushed them together.

She didn't say anything, just stood there, trembling.

"It's okay." Regina took a step toward her, her arm raised, ready to touch her shoulder.

The rumble of a group broke their silence. They were coming their way. The look of sorrow on the girl's face turned into terror.

"No, they're coming." The girl said the words like she was pleading for mercy. "No, please!" Tears dripped onto her cheeks.

"It's oka—" Regina didn't get to console her. Between two moments, or two blinks perhaps, the girl disappeared from Regina's sight, and the only thing Regina's arm reached was air.

Regina turned around to look for her, but she only saw what the girl had left behind—the drawing in the dust. It was not even a drawing, but two letters, connected with a plus sign. She must have traced them over and over: M+N.

The source of the rumble appeared on the path—a group of skull-carriers. The same group Regina had met before. They stopped at a safe distance from Regina and stared at her in silence.

"Do you know what kind of eyes dragons have?" asked a small boy. His voice was high, and he had a lisp.

"All-seeing?" Regina raised her eyebrows.

"Exactly," said another boy, this one older. "Their tears must help their eyes see so well."

Regina considered this for a moment, but didn't get anywhere. "What?"

"Dragons see things people can't," said the boy. "Their *tears* must help their eyes see so well."

Regina narrowed her eyes as she looked at the strangely stiff group in front of her. All their looks felt heavy on her.

"Their tears must help their eyes see so well," said a girl with curly blonde hair.

"Their tears must help their eyes see so well," a red-haired boy repeated.

"Their tears must help their eyes see so well," the whole group chanted like they were saying some kind of spell. "Their tears must help their eyes see so well. Their tears must help their eyes see so well. Their tears must help their eyes see so well."

Regina woke up in a cold sweat. Again.

10. THE TOWN THAT STOOD ALONE

Regina sat on her bed, gasping for air. Brunorth rested his head on her shoulder, letting her know he was there.

When Regina's breathing finally slowed down, she lowered her forehead into her palm.

"Their tears must help their eyes see so well," she said to herself, her voice tired. She looked at Brunorth. "What does that mean? You see things I can't. Your tears help you see?" Regina searched the dragon's face with a frown, but her eyes opened wide when it all clicked inside her mind. "Dragontears!" she exclaimed and was already searching for the article under her pillow. "They were talking about the Dragontears!"

With the piece of paper in her hand, she jumped out of bed and rushed to the closest plant that had grown all over the wall. Its light was warm and calming. Outside, the sun was just starting to come up.

Regina lifted the article in front of it so it could shine through the paper. And the missing words appeared.

LOSTHAN BRINGS JUSTICE FOR THE WEAK!
Weakness Lowborn (13) was found dead in Initiation Orphanage on Tuesday. She was holding a photo of her brother, Malformed Lowborn (17), which Losthan rule enforcers believe was the girl's way to reveal her killer. Other residents of the institution described Malformed as violent, saying he is as rotten on the inside as he is on the outside. Losthan shall not stand for violence against the weak! The one responsible will be severely punished!

Regina's mouth fell open. Her heart was beating in her throat. She had to swallow to make the throbbing go away.

She looked out the window. The sun was slowly waking up.

Regina got dressed in such a hurry that it wouldn't have been surprising if she wore a shirt instead of pants, but maybe thanks to some kind of Andarian miracle, she managed to dress up properly.

Brunorth almost couldn't catch up with her, she left the hut so suddenly. She rushed across the Field of Cetana, and even a minute couldn't pass, she was already knocking on Joey's door.

When Joey opened the door, Regina didn't even wait for him to say anything, she rushed in and placed the article in front of the Dragontears on Joey's wall.

"Come, read it," she said.

"Dragontears make the words appear? Why didn't we try that? And how did you know?" Joey made his way toward Regina, petting Brunorth in the process.

"I had a dream again. With the skull-carriers. They kind of told me. In the creepiest way possible. Oh." Regina lowered the article just when Joey was about to read it. "And I saw the girl too. Who looks like me. The girl in the picture."

"In your dream?"

"Yes. She's a skull-carrier too."

"So she did die," said Joey, a bit disappointed.

"Yeah." Regina lifted the article in the warm light again and let Joey read the story.

"Malformed Lowborn?" Joey frowned. "What kind of

name is that, geez."

"They name everyone like that in Losthan," said Regina, remembering what she had learned in school. "They look at a newborn and give them a name based on what they think. If they think someone will grow up to be strong, they name them Strength. If someone is really ugly, they name them Ugly. And there are only two possible surnames: Lowborn and Highborn. Most of the people in Losthan are Lowborn, meaning they are born into poverty. There are only a couple of families that have the Highborn name. They live in houses of gold and stuff like that."

"Yeah, I remember now," said Joey and finished reading the article. "She's his sister," he said, still looking at the piece of paper. "The girl who looks like you. She was Weakness."

"Ness. That's what Mal called me. That's why he thought he knew me."

"And he might have killed her." Joey searched the picture with his eyes like he was hoping the girl would jump out of the paper and tell them what had happened to her.

"They're orphans." Regina tried to gather the information they had. But all this was not easy on her heart.

Joey sighed and looked at Regina. His eyes were heavy

with a pain that was not his. "This is the life he has to remember."

Regina was on the verge of shedding tears. Her face scrunched up like there was an ache in her body. "I—I don't know what to say."

"There's nothing much to say, really." Joey looked out the window. The sun had already climbed into the sky. "Not everyone in the world is from Tupsbade, like us, where most people are pretty well-off." He was talking more to himself than to Regina. "In some parts of the world *this* is . . . average." He gestured toward the article with a disillusioned motion.

"So it's possible Mal is a killer," said Regina.

"Yep." Joey still stood, looking out the window.

"And he might have killed . . . all those kids in my dream."

"Yep."

People came to Andara from everywhere. Even from a town that didn't seem real to the rest of the world.

Because Losthan was a part of the normal world, their world, their home, but wasn't a part of it at the same time. It stood alone. With all of its atrocities, all of its secrets and all of its pain that the rest of the world could only guess at.

Regina plopped into the nearest chair. She couldn't even begin to imagine what a child of Losthan was like. She had met Mal, she had looked into his eyes, but she didn't know him. She couldn't know him. Because even though they were from the same planet, the not so ordinary boy was from a completely different world.

11: THE MAN IN THE DAPPER SUIT

Regina and Joey couldn't do much about the issues concerning Mal. They couldn't do anything, actually.

Mal was in the middle of his journey through Andara somewhere, and Regina or Joey couldn't touch what choices he would make, what memories he would remember or what kind of person he was under all of that.

So to take Regina's mind off things—and her head *really* needed a break—Joey suggested a walk.

"Do you think there are parts of Andara we haven't seen?" Regina asked as they were walking across the field, toward Dara Forest.

"Probably," said Joey. "I'm pretty sure there are a lot of creatures too that we haven't met. Like the mermaid. You remember?"

"How could I forget . . . ?" Regina thought back to the screaming mermaid who had jumped out of the water while they were crossing the narrow path to Mount Napharata. "I wonder what purpose they serve here."

Joey shrugged. "They must be here for a reason."

The leaves of the old trees shielded them from the sun as they stepped into the forest.

Regina heard something crack behind them, like someone stepped on a dry branch, but she didn't turn. She didn't want to notice. She didn't want to feel like someone was watching her. And she certainly didn't want to turn around and see a dark silhouette somewhere among the trees. At that moment, it was easier to ignore the sound like it had never happened. Joey didn't seem to notice, or maybe he didn't want to notice either.

"Are you starting to miss home?" asked Regina, out of the blue.

Joey pursed his lips. "Not really. I'm kind of glad to be away for a bit, actually. I used to wish I could stop time and just step out of my life for a little bit, you know? This is sort of like that. It's exactly like that, actually. I'm happy to be here." He flashed a smile at Regina.

Regina shot a smile back before she lowered her eyes to the ground in front of her feet. She knew Joey had a difficult family situation back home, his father being a violent drunk and his mother refusing to leave him regardless, always siding with her husband, even when Joey had to be the one to protect her from him.

It was not hard to understand why he was glad to be away from all that for a little while. Why he had even fantasized about stopping time. Regina had her own problems in her family, but she had never wished to stop time and step out of life for a little bit. She couldn't imagine what that must have been like.

She glanced at Joey. His warm brown eyes glowed in a beam of sunlight, making them caramel-colored. A small half-smile sat on his face that seemed permanent to Regina at this point as he looked up into the light seeping in between the trees.

Regina wished he would never have to go back to that place. But then again, it was still better than Joey staying in Andara forever and becoming a Living Dead. In that moment, Regina understood the Living Dead and why people chose to never go back home. She had never really thought about it before.

"Step right up, ladies and gentlemen, for the best location in Andara." The unusual voice broke Regina's train of thought. It was the voice of a man—smooth and cunning, like he knew a secret they didn't.

Regina and Joey turned to look at the speaker. A man stood among the trees—unusually tall, unusually slim and unusually sleek. The black of his dapper suit glinted in the sunlight.

The man was leaning against one of the trees, his hands in the pockets of his spotless pants. He looked at them with sharp eyes that were a bit narrowed like a panther's stalking its prey. His slicked-back hair glinted, much like his suit.

He didn't seem like someone who lived in a forest. He looked like someone who had never even stepped foot in a forest, actually. His exterior was too dirt-free, too well-groomed, too *perfect* for that. And yet, there he stood, in the middle of Dara Forest, untouched by all that lay around him.

"Step right up," the man repeated. He didn't shout at all, he spoke calmly and quietly, like he was doing the world a favor by showing them whatever he wanted them to step up to.

The man looked so fancy that Regina didn't even think he was talking to them. Someone that elegant wouldn't even talk to people like them.

But when she looked around, no one else was in sight, so she pointed at herself, confused. "Us?"

"Well, who else is there?" the man said, his voice still effortless and quiet. He pushed himself away from the tree and began walking away. He looked like a dark wave of the ocean as his slender body moved.

Regina and Joey looked at each other.

"I think he wants us to follow him," said Joey.

"The creepy guy in the forest?" Regina raised an eyebrow.

Joey shrugged. "We've got Brunorth."

Regina looked down at the dragon who was suspiciously eyeing the man.

"And a Nayaka too." Joey winked.

Regina smiled then shrugged. "Okay, if you say so. Whoever this guy is, we've probably seen worse already."

Regina, Joey and Brunorth started after the slender man. Regina couldn't take her eyes off of the way his suit glistened in the sunlight. The way it moved on his frame slowly, like the calm ripples of the ocean . . . It would have been so easy to just . . . fall into it . . . let it cover her like a blanket—safe and warm . . .

"This is the Tunnel," the man said matter-of-factly.

Regina didn't even notice he had stopped and turned toward them. She had to blink a couple of times to bring herself back to the present moment. The man stood next to a sad pile of leaves.

"This is the best location in Andara." The man talked like he was bored. Almost as if he was doing *them* a favor. "The only *safe* one." He nodded slowly and looked at them deeply as he let those words sink in. "Let me ask you a question." He pushed his fingers together. "Do you feel safe?"

Regina and Joey glanced at each other.

"Yeah." Joey shrugged.

"I mean, sure," Regina said, half-lying.

The man ran his hand across his chin like he was stroking an invisible beard. "That's where you're wrong," he said. "You are not safe. In fact, you are in *constant* danger." He reached into his suit and pulled out two white cards. They were just as shiny as his suit. "That's where I come in," he said, holding the cards between two fingers and handing them to Regina and Joey.

"The Shadow Man, at your service."

12 · THE LOGICAL DECISION

Regina took the card from the Shadow Man's hand.

THE SHADOW MAN

Keeping humans safe since the beginning of time.

Regina flipped the card around, but nothing else was written on it.

"Shouldn't a business card have a phone number or something?" she said. "You can't do business unless you can reach the person." She looked at the Shadow Man with one raised eyebrow.

The man grinned, and Regina could have sworn his eyes glinted maliciously.

"Oh, but my card *is* how you can contact me." He tilted

his head and looked down at Regina. "All you have to do is look at it and want me to save you. And I'll be there before you can even shout for help."

"So you're like a protector of some sort?" asked Joey.

"You could say that, yes." The man stroked his imaginary beard again. "In this chaos that is Andara, I'm the only one who wants to keep humans safe. The only one who *can* keep them safe." He spoke as if he was feeling sorry for all his poor, defenseless human friends. "After all, what happens if you get sick?" He leaned into Regina's face with a worried expression that seemed a bit artificial. Like he was trying to sell them something. "What if you get lost? What if you get hurt? What if *someone* hurts you?"

Regina and Joey didn't know the answer.

"Your Andarian friends will not help you. You're only important to them as long as you're fine, healthy, *perfect*, as long as you are able to stand on their side." He paced left and right in front of them, looking like he wanted to spit on the ground, but resisted. Someone in a suit like that couldn't behave like such a brute, after all. "They all want humans for their own selfish gains, but what have they ever done for you?"

96

Regina was about to open her mouth to answer, but the Shadow Man was already in her face, pushing his finger in front of her lips. "Don't say a word," he whispered then turned around dramatically with his forearm on his forehead. "It pains me to hear the delusions they brainwashed you with."

Regina looked at Joey with eyebrows raised high. Joey shrugged with a smile.

"But don't let me convince you." The Shadow Man turned back toward them. He stood straight, his fingers pushed together, his voice slow and quiet. "That's what the Tunnel is for." He lifted his hands toward the sad pile of leaves behind him.

"Are you trying to sell us something?" Joey asked with narrow eyes. "Just because we don't have any mo—"

"No, boy." The Shadow Man interrupted calmly. His face was stern like a rock. "What I offer never needed to be forced on anyone. Humans come to me. Just like you have." His eyes never left Regina's, and somehow, she was sure that they never left Joey's either. If someone was capable of looking into two people's eyes at the same time, this guy was it. Regina just now noticed that since she had been looking at him, he hadn't blinked once.

Regina swallowed. Fear began creeping up her throat, even though she didn't understand why. She couldn't take her eyes off of the Shadow Man. She felt like something horrible would happen to her if she did.

As she looked into his eyes, which were an infinite black, like his suit, she understood that she needed to step into the pile of leaves. An inexplicable feeling took over her that convinced her that the pile of leaves was the only place she would be safe.

It was like someone was after her that she needed to hide from. Which *was* true, now that she thought about it. Mal was probably still lurking in the woods somewhere, spying on her, preparing to do who-knows-what to her. Yes, she needed to step into the leaves to hide from him. The Shadow Man came to protect her from him.

As if Joey was having the same exact feelings and thoughts, they stepped toward the pile of leaves in unison. Regina didn't know what Brunorth was doing. She didn't hear him next to her. It didn't matter. She needed to step into the leaves.

Stepping into a pile a leaves didn't seem like a stupid

idea, it didn't even seem unusual or weird. It made perfect sense in Regina's mind. In that moment, it was the most logical choice of all. So that's what she did.

With Joey by her side moving almost exactly like she moved, they stepped into the pile. But the leaves didn't crunch or tear beneath their feet, they didn't even make a sound. Instead of standing in a pile of foliage like two confused children, they fell like the leaves had not been leaves at all. Like they were only an illusion of leaves that were hiding a trap.

A trap in the middle of the forest, set by the strange man in a dapper suit.

As she was falling, Regina didn't feel like she had made a bad decision. The Tunnel was where she was supposed to be. It would bring her security. It would keep her safe.

The Shadow Man would keep her safe. As she was falling through the darkness, she imagined the strange man in her mind. When he had turned his back on them, Regina could have sworn that she saw a tail sticking out from under his fine suit. A red tail, kind of like a demon's, that he tried to hide under his jacket.

Regina was scared. But strangely, not because she was

falling into the trap of an unusual man with a demon's tail. *That* didn't worry her at all for some reason.

It would have been logical to question the goodwill of a man in a suit so neat, it didn't even carry one wrinkle or speck of dust in the middle of the forest. Not to mention the demon's tail he was trying to hide. Yes, those might have been causes of concern for a logical person. But the Tunnel was not a logical place at all.

13. A BAD FEELING

Regina stood somewhere familiar. She had been here before—only not when awake. Regina stood on the underground pathway, tree roots dangling above her head.

In her dreams, Regina had met many souls here whose lives had ended. She had always wondered if the underground pathway actually existed somewhere in Andara. Now, she was standing there, flesh and bone, on the pathway she had walked through many times in her dreams—the Tunnel.

But the Tunnel was not like in her dreams at all. It didn't *look* that much different. But it *felt* like a completely different place.

One possible reason for that was probably that the path was not empty this time. The roots of trees weren't the only things softly moving in the Tunnel.

People trod along the sides of the path. Or maybe they were not people at all—not humans. Regina couldn't see their faces; pieces of black lace covered them. All of their clothes looked like they were on their way to a funeral.

Some had flowers in their hands—black flowers that had withered long ago. Others were clutching onto picture frames or random little tokens.

Regina stood and watched the sad black figures. Here, in the Tunnel, she didn't feel much. Still, she started to have a bad feeling. The grieving figures were all walking toward her. It was almost like all these people were mourning . . . something about *her*.

The bad feeling in Regina's stomach intensified. She tried to swallow, but there wasn't much moisture left in her mouth.

Then a small sense shot back into Regina's mind, which didn't seem to operate correctly since she had entered the Tunnel, and she remembered Joey. They had stepped into the pile of leaves together.

Regina looked around. The boy was nowhere. Neither was Brunorth. The dragon hadn't fallen into the pile of leaves with them, she remembered faintly.

"Joey?" Regina said as loudly as she could, but still trying not to attract the attention of the marching mourners. She succeeded, because they didn't seem to hear her at all. They kept walking their slow, grave walk toward her.

"Regina?" Joey's voice was like an echo coming from a neighboring tunnel.

"Joey, where are you?"

"I don't know, this tunnel is so small."

Regina looked at the path in front of her. She wouldn't have called the tunnel she was standing in small. If anything, it was quite wide.

Joey was not seeing the same thing she was.

"Do you also see all these people?"

"What people?"

"The people in black? The people . . . mourning?"

After a short silence Joey said, "No."

Regina tried to swallow again, but the dryness of her throat only made her cough.

She rubbed her eyes, trying to get her mind to work, but she couldn't think a single straight thought.

"Are you okay? They aren't hurting you, are they?" Joey's voice became more distant, more distorted and faint as Regina tried to get a grip.

"No," she said, narrowing her eyes.

There was no other way, only forward.

"Is there enough room for you to walk?" Regina was

glad she could scrape her brain cells back into place a bit and comprehend Joey's situation.

"Yeah." Joey didn't sound as disoriented as Regina felt. He didn't sound fazed at all. Maybe it was a Nayaka thing.

"Then let's see what this place is about," said Regina, her voice a bit confused. She wasn't loud, but she knew Joey heard her.

Regina began walking forward. She didn't see the Shadow Man, but she felt his card in her pocket. She knew he was not far away at all.

When Regina reached the two lines of mourners walking on the sides of the path, she hesitated to step between them. The empty way they had left just for Regina was eagerly waiting for her. Regina didn't even try to swallow at this point.

She looked back—there was no other way. She had to step between them. So she did.

Her confused mind didn't expect much to happen. All she had inside was a bad feeling.

Nothing happened. But now that Regina could look at the mourners more closely, she saw that their mouths—the only thing not covered by black lace—were moving. They were mumbling. And Regina now heard their sad voices full of suffering.

She didn't understand what they were saying; she couldn't hear the words coming out of their mouths. But she couldn't avoid feeling the hurt coming from their painful tones. Like all these people had to endure suffering she couldn't even imagine.

In a moment of clarity, compassion sneaked into Regina's heart for the mourners around her, full of hurt.

"I'm so sorry for your loss," she heard herself say, even though she didn't know where the words had come from.

Like they heard a faint sound, the mourners stopped in their steps. Both lines stood still.

As if they hadn't moved their necks in a long time, they lifted their heads like statues trying to come to life. Searching for the source of the voice they had heard, they moved like very, very old people—or maybe people that had not been alive for a long time, and now they were trying to come to life.

Regina's blinks were rapid as she watched them. There was nowhere to run.

Slowly, all faces found Regina. She could feel their eyes

drilling into her. Even if they didn't have eyes under the black lace, Regina knew they *sensed* her. They knew she was there.

And just like that, the mourning began.

14 MOURNING

The mourner standing closest to Regina looked like a granny under all the layers of black lace. She held a withered bouquet of flowers in her hand and began lifting the other one toward Regina. Just like their necks, her hand moved like she hadn't used it in decades.

The lace slipped off the mourner's arm—there was nothing on her bones except for old skin as gray as death, withered just like the flowers she was holding. The fingers reaching toward Regina were fragile bones—faded ghosts of a human hand.

Then this strange being touched Regina's arm. And Regina just stood there, staring at the paper-like skin covered with moles and warts. The mourner's touch was neither hot nor cold. It just *was*, sitting there on Regina's skin like an unnatural growth, spreading something in her body that could only be labeled as *dread*.

Dread so powerful, there could never be any cause for a person to feel it. Even facing death itself wouldn't call for such a feeling. But Regina was standing in the Tunnel. And the Tunnel was not a logical place.

So Regina didn't yank her arm away. She just stared at it and let the bony fingers fester on her skin.

Then the mourner spoke like she was exhaling her last breath.

"You have"—her voice was raspy and strained, like her throat was as thirsty as her paper skin—"already lost."

Dread flexed its muscles. Regina forced a breath down. Not enough air. Not nearly enough.

"The child of Losthan will find you. They always do."

Regina saw it in front of her eyes like it was actually happening—the children of Losthan. She watched them beat each other with sticks, hurt animals, set buildings on fire.

There was only one thing she could think:

Savages. All of them.

Regina blinked so rapidly, she didn't even notice another

mourner had shuffled next to her—his hand was already on her arm, bony fingers sticking out of the black lace suit he was wearing. He was clutching a gold picture frame with a black and white photo of a girl. A girl with a smile as bright as a thousand suns. Regina knew her. She had seen the exact same photo above the news of the girl's death—Ness.

"Your fate's the same as hers." The man's voice sounded like he had a throat infection no one could cure. "Such tragedy. Such misfortune." He hugged the picture and cried like he was at a funeral.

Regina saw it in front of her eyes: A boy with a deformed face laughing his evil laugh like a demon, like a ghoul, like a killer. *He looks like a monster because he is one.*

"All monsters are human." Another mourner was touching Regina now.

As Regina turned her head, she couldn't see anything else—only face after face covered in black lace, staring at her with hidden eyes. Their gray and cracked lips spat words of mourning, growing that powerful feeling of fear inside Regina.

Dread now stood above all else as an undefeated champion. Even if there was nothing there to conquer.

"My child was a loving soul, and she died at the hands of an uncivilized brute from Losthan," a woman's dying voice cried. Regina couldn't see which pair of lips were moving among the many similar faces. "They are all monsters. They are. Not like us at all."

"My sister is gone because of a monster with a deformed face. Nothing is a coincidence, nothing. The almighty marked him for a reason." The man's voice was filled with pain and suffering. It hurt Regina's stomach just to listen to him.

"My friend," breathed a girl, "my friend suffered so much. She was in so much pain. She was a victim. A victim."

A victim. A victim. A victim.

I am a victim.

Dread shook its fists in the air in triumph. It had won.

Regina felt impending doom rise above her like a stormy cloud. All this pain and suffering—it was waiting for *her*. But it was all too much for her to carry.

She tried to search for something around her, anything that wasn't a face covered by black lace. But she couldn't see anything else. Only face after face after face whispering ghoulish secrets that were impossible not to believe. Because down here, in the Tunnel, they all made sense.

Even if Joey spoke to her, she couldn't hear him anymore. His voice got smothered by mourning.

There was nothing left, only grief for a future not yet lived. And that kind of grief was the hardest to bear.

I am a victim.

And just like that, it dawned on Regina: The child with a loving soul, the sister gone because of a monster, the friend who suffered so much—they were all . . . her. All these faces covered in black lace were in mourning because of her.

This was her funeral.

15: FALLING TREES AND A PERFECT DOOR

No. No. No. No. I don't want to be here. I have to get out of here. I have to get out of here.

Regina kept her eyes squeezed shut. She didn't want to see all the eyeless faces looking at her. Staring deep into her. Knowing things about her future she didn't want to know. But now, she would never be able to forget.

Mal would find her and do who-knows-what to her. He was a monster. A barbaric child of Losthan. He had killed his own sister and all those kids. She couldn't hide.

There was no way out. She was surrounded by lace-covered faces pushed so closely together, even a fly couldn't fit through them.

But Regina had to get out of here. The urge to flee was as strong in her as in a wounded antelope surrounded by lions.

But what could she do? How could she get out of this lightless tunnel? She tried to think, but her brain didn't cooperate.

In an attempt to hide as much of herself as she could, she stuffed her hands deeply inside her pockets. Her eyes popped open when she felt it—the Shadow Man's card. It was ice cold between her fingers. Or maybe Regina's hand was burning hot.

Either way, she slid it out of her pants and looked at it, trying to avoid the faces surrounding her.

THE SHADOW MAN

Keeping humans safe since the beginning of time.

The white card shone strangely in the darkness. Not in a beautiful way like the Dragontears outside, more like ivory made from the tusk of an elephant, taken forcibly by hunters.

Regina breathed heavily as she held the card in her hand like it was the only thing that could save her.

"Keep me safe," she breathed. "Please." She shut her

eyes. Maybe because she feared what would happen. Maybe because she feared nothing would.

When she opened them again, the faces were gone. Regina let out half of a sigh. Not a full sigh—she was still in the Tunnel.

The sudden touch of a hand on her shoulder made her stiffen and hold her breath. The touch was not harsh or violent by any means. It was slow and smooth. Too slow. Too smooth.

Regina didn't move, but she saw the hand from the corner of her eye. In the darkness, the skin looked gray, but something gold shone above it repulsively—a cufflink on the wrinkle-free sleeve of a white shirt peeking out from under a black suit jacket.

"You called?" The Shadow Man's voice smiled, but not with kindness or joy—it smiled with the love of another's vulnerability.

"Somewhere safe. Take me somewhere safe," Regina said, still not looking at the owner of the hand on her shoulder. "Make it stop. Make it end. I just want to be safe. I just want to feel good again." She closed her eyes, suffering, but even through her shut eyelids, she could somehow see the man's teeth glint in a wide grin somewhere behind her.

"Very well," he said, and gave Regina's shoulder a little pull. "Right this way." His voice was calm and quiet, but Regina didn't relax from it. She still sensed something malicious behind the façade of perfection. But there was no better options available to her right now. And she had no doubt in her mind about the Shadow Man's abilities to keep her safe.

He would keep her safe. He would. But if he would, why couldn't Regina relax?

The Shadow Man guided Regina with gentle pushes and pulls through the Tunnel. Regina didn't want to look anywhere, she didn't want to see anything from this place, so she kept looking down, watching her dirty shoes stupidly *step, step, step* where the man was leading them.

She could still see from the corner of her eye that the roots of the trees above her were dangling like octopus arms. *What if the trees fall? What if the ground collapses and dozens of trees come crashing down?* Regina stumbled—the Shadow Man had to grab her other shoulder with his other hand to keep her on her feet.

"The trees are going to fall," she said, her voice more

like a cry than speech. She hid her face inside her palms.

"You will be safe in the Room of Comfort," said the Shadow Man, softly guiding her on. "We are here already. You will be safe here."

Regina lowered her hands. She was on the verge of crying, but she couldn't afford to cry. Not in a situation this serious.

They had stopped in front of a door in the side of the Tunnel. It was a beautiful lavender color—Regina's favorite. In the middle, sparkling silver letters revealed what the door hid: ROOM OF COMFORT. Under it, almost unnoticeable, white words added: ENTRY OPTIONAL. Just the sight of the door made Regina feel like this was the place where she could finally relax.

The Shadow Man placed his hand on the fancy silver door handle. This door looked brand new, untouched—*perfect*. It looked like it didn't belong here. And a place that didn't have anything to do with the Tunnel was exactly where Regina wanted to be.

But the Shadow Man didn't push the handle down. His hand just rested on it like a perfect, gray, lifeless glove.

Regina stared at it in anticipation. She bit the inside of

her cheek. She shifted her weight. She was starting to lose it. Didn't the Shadow Man understand her life was on the line?

She tried to bite her tongue, but the words escaped her mouth anyway. "Let me in!" she yelled suddenly at the Shadow Man.

The Shadow Man grinned, like Regina's outburst was exactly what he had been waiting for.

"Your wish is my command," he said and opened the door wide.

16. THE SHADOW MAN'S CURRENCY

The walls were beige inside the room with a bit of silver glitter sparkling on them. The ceiling was clean white and the flooring soft brown wood.

The room was fully furnished: a brand new bed in one corner, a vanity in the other, a bookcase against a wall, and a large TV mounted onto another, facing a fluffy couch in the middle of the room—all of it white. Pillows and cute stuffed animals decorated almost everything and pictures of flowers, rainbows and other cute things hung on the walls. Everything was clean and soft and perfect.

The Shadow Man closed the door behind them. The TV was on, Regina's favorite childhood cartoon playing on it. Finally, a place where Regina could relax. A place where she was safe—the Room of Comfort.

Regina sighed without the breath hurting her dry throat. She let herself fall onto the couch, burying her face into the soft cushions.

The intro song of her favorite cartoon filled the room. She let herself listen to it. It used to always calm her as a child—when her parents were fighting, when they had lost all interest to fight, when her brother hit her or when he told her that she was the cause of everything falling apart.

The magical girls in the cartoon didn't say such things about her. They didn't say mean words to anyone, not even the villains. Instead of killing them, they helped them get better. Regina always wanted to be like them. Watching the cartoon, she felt like she could be.

"Such an interesting tale this is." The Shadow Man had sat down on the couch, next to Regina. He seemed to follow Regina like . . . well, a shadow. With one arm thrown across the backrest, he watched the TV with curiosity.

"It used to be my favorite show," said Regina, sitting up. She sank into the couch—it was as soft as a cloud.

"I know," the Shadow Man said, like it was obvious. "Why do you think it's on?" He glanced at Regina with raised brows.

"Oh." Regina suddenly realized that this room was the Shadow Man's doing. He had created this room specifically for her. It was her very own room of comfort. "Thank you."

"Nothing to thank. It's what I do."

Regina tried to sneak a peek at the Shadow Man without him noticing. The suit on him was still as wrinkle-free as ever, his white shirt and suit jacket perfectly aligned.

Regina lowered her eyes to his waist, trying to determine if the demon tail she had seen was there. Nothing was sticking out, but there was definitely something hidden under his suit jacket.

"Why though?" Regina said.

"Why what?"

"Why do you help people? Keep them safe?"

A grin stretched across the Shadow Man's face. "I don't seem like someone who just . . . helps people?" He adjusted his gold cufflinks. "Out of the goodness of my heart?"

"Not really," said Regina, plain and simple. She had gotten so tired, there was no energy left in her to consider the feelings of unusual creatures.

The Shadow Man stood up and began leisurely walking around the room, hands placed behind his back. "I'm a businessman. Not like the businessmen in your world though." He said that with contempt. Like he was above humans in some way. "I'm the *original* businessman, if you will. The *best*."

"So, do you want money?" Regina asked, quite sure that the best businessman in the two worlds was aware that a thirteen-year-old girl didn't have any money to give.

"Oh, no, no." The Shadow Man smiled a smile that made Regina feel like he knew something she didn't. "Money is the obsession of the weak. And as I said, I am the best." He raised one eyebrow. "I have no interest in useless things."

"Why do you do it then? And where did you get that suit?"

The Shadow Man laughed. "This, my dear"—he touched the shiny material of his jacket—"is not something you could ever come across in the other world. It's something only I can possess." He paused and looked at Regina with sharp eyes for a moment. "It's also why I do what I do."

Regina gathered her brows. She looked more closely at the black material the Shadow Man was holding between his hands. The black seemed endless . . . like there were infinite worlds inside of his suit. "What is that?"

The Shadow Man smoothed down his jacket. "It's no fun if I tell you. Guess." He stood straight, every feature on him sharp and dark, like the black of his suit.

Regina tried to decide what the infinite something inside of his suit might have been, but she couldn't think of anything. "I don't know."

"It's the most powerful feeling in the world." He poked some stuffed animals with his sharp finger. "The thing that makes one feel like *different* means *dangerous*. The thing that erases the world around you, leaving you alone and terrified. The thing that destroys cities, lives, families. Something of which you humans have endless amounts." He pulled his hand across his jacket like he was stroking his suit. "Your weakness becomes my power. It's my very own currency, if you will."

Regina still didn't understand what he was talking about. If anything, she was even more confused. The Shadow Man was the one who kept humans safe, was he not? Then why was he talking about destroyed cities and lives? She didn't get it. Of course she didn't. She was still inside the Tunnel, after all.

"Tell me," she said. "I will have to give it to you too, won't I? You helped me."

"Oh, my dear," said the Shadow Man, walking up to the TV, "you already have."

It was out in the open now, maybe it had been all along, Regina just couldn't see—a red tail moving left and right, coming from under the dapper suit.

Regina glanced at the TV. Her cartoon would make her feel calm again. But the magical girls were being beaten by the villains. And the Shadow Man just smiled.

They sat there, in the perfect room, the sound of the television being the only thing disrupting the silence.

Slowly, like a snake creeping up her leg, Regina started to feel uneasy again. Like the feeling she had left outside the door was slithering right back inside her.

She took her eyes off the TV. She tried to concentrate on her breathing. But the snake of unease continued climbing up her legs. It encircled her waist then her chest and finally, her throat. It didn't matter how much she wanted to concentrate on her breathing when she felt like she was going to be sick, faint and choke at the same time.

She sat up, gasping for air.

124

She would be an easy victim for Mal in this state. She wouldn't even be able to run away if he threw a lit match right at her feet.

Dread flushed over Regina like a tidal wave—it was back, stronger than ever. Maybe it had never left. She hunched forward, trying to make herself as small as she could.

The Shadow Man's intention was never to help her. He just wanted to make her . . . pay him. In his very own currency.

She knew it now, but there was no stopping the feeling. The feeling she knew was only adding to the infinite blackness of the wrinkle-free suit.

"You understand now, don't you?" the Shadow Man whispered in her ear. "You sure have a lot to offer me, Regina. And I can offer you safety in return. It's a fair trade, don't you think?"

Regina stayed hunched over on the couch, bearing the whisper that made her skin crawl. Her mind was too clouded to determine what she needed to do.

She tried desperately to calm herself, but couldn't. And the fact that she couldn't, made her feel even worse. Guilty, sad, *terrified.*

She understood now what the Shadow Man's currency was—it was the choking feeling inside of her she couldn't get rid of. The blackness that created infinite worlds inside of his perfectly disturbing suit . . . was fear.

17 PERFECTION

"I don't want to feel this," Regina cried into her palms, still hunched over on the perfectly soft couch.

"The world is a scary place," the Shadow Man said. "Humans are dangerous creatures."

Regina closed her eyes. She didn't want to hear him. She didn't want to hear the cartoon on the television. She just wanted all the noise to quiet down—outside and inside of her head.

But it wasn't that easy. If there was no danger, then why was she so utterly terrified? There must have been a reason for all this upheaval inside of her.

She didn't want to leave the safety of this room. Even though she felt horrible, it was better than dying. And if she left, Mal would find her and do who-knows-what to her. He

127

couldn't be trusted. He was strange, different, *unknown*. Yes, even sitting in this horrible terror was better than having to deal with him.

She could even wish herself back home if she wanted, but she was not going to leave Andara because of some strange kid who probably shouldn't have even come here in the first place. He didn't even have any memories about who he was or what he was doing in Andara.

Regina sighed into her palms. All of these thoughts were very unlike her. There had been a couple of instances when she felt like her head wasn't on straight, like after hearing something terrible on the news or sometimes when a memory of her absent father came to her mind. But they had all passed, and she survived. So why did it feel like this feeling was never going to end?

She straightened up. Slowly, she looked at the Shadow Man, sitting next to her. He rested his eyes on her with a smug smile on his face, like a businessman who had just made the biggest sale in his career.

"I changed my mind," said Regina, trying to keep her voice from shaking. "I won't be needing your services. Please let me out of here."

The Shadow Man just smiled without a word.

"Let me out of here," Regina repeated, her voice more heavy this time.

But the Shadow Man just smiled.

"Don't you hear me?" Regina stood up. Dizziness made her stumble. "I don't need your services!"

"There's nothing to be done once I've already been paid," the Shadow Man said simply.

Regina started looking around the room. There was no reasoning with this demon or whatever he was.

Regina ran to the door. She tried to push the handle down, but it was no use—it didn't even move one bit.

There must have been a way out of this place. Regina ran to the fluffy bed filled with stuffed animals and threw them on the floor, along with the pillows and the duvet—all in Regina's favorite shade. Under all of it lay a perfectly normal bed.

She pulled the bed aside—maybe a trap door or something hid under it. But there was nothing there, only perfectly normal floorboards.

She moved the bookcase and the vanity too, but no escape route presented itself anywhere. All the while, the feeling of fainting, throwing up, going crazy and dying, possibly all at the same time, maybe one after another, swirled around inside of her like a bad lunch.

The Shadow Man stayed on the couch, watching the cartoon with one arm thrown across the backrest. He sat there like it didn't matter what Regina would do. Like they had already made a silent deal, and there was no escaping from it.

Regina knew now that it was useless to search for a way out. She stared at the back of the Shadow Man's head with eyes filling up with tears. Every strand of his hair was perfectly combed into place. It made Regina's stomach turn. Even more than it already had.

"Why are you doing this?" she asked in a dying voice.

The Shadow Man turned off the TV, even though Regina didn't see a remote in his hand. He stood up, arms placed behind his back. His red tail was fully visible now, and Regina wasn't even surprised.

"It's my job," he said simply. "It's not so pleasant. To carry all this around." He glanced at his suit.

"I thought you were proud of it," Regina said between two gasps. "Being the best businessman in the two worlds and all. That's what you said."

The Shadow Man just stared at her in silence for a moment that seemed like the longest quiet moment ever to Regina.

"I say a lot of things." The Shadow Man was next to Regina, but she hadn't even seen him take a step. "Maybe it would be better if you just . . . left."

Regina took a couple steps back. She looked at the Shadow Man as if she were looking at a madman. "What are you talking about? You said the exact opposite a minute ago! What do you want?" The Shadow Man's opposing statements didn't help her feel saner.

"Nothing produces more energy than a human who is utterly and totally terrified. And I *love* that power." His voice suddenly got higher. "I *do*." He turned his back to Regina. "But sometimes . . . it gets a little too much."

"What do you mean?" Regina straightened up, starting to get concerned about the Shadow Man.

"All I'm saying is"—the Shadow Man turned back toward her with eyebrows raised—"that you have free will. That is all." He was right next to Regina again, even though he hadn't moved. "Use it," he whispered into her ear.

Regina stumbled backward. All the tension, the anxiety, the fear inside of her—it had become unbearable. And in that moment, Regina's biggest problem was not Mal anymore, but her own feelings.

And the Room of Comfort was not going to take her feelings away.

"This really feels horrible," she said with a painful smile.

"I know exactly how it feels, believe me." The Shadow Man's voice was no longer fiendish—it was tired and sad. "You might be safe here. You might not be."

"What is making you say these things?" Regina said, half laughing, half crying.

"What's making me say it is that"—he appeared right in front of Regina's face, looking deep into her eyes—"I *really* want your fear." He sounded like fear was food and he hadn't eaten in weeks. He disappeared and reappeared in the farthest corner of the room. "But I *really* don't want it at the same time. It's *heavy*."

"I might not be safe out there," said Regina, fed up with it all, "but I'm not going to hide in this room with you. I don't care anymore."

"Are you sure?" The Shadow Man's voice was higher

again, and his hands were lifted in front of his mouth like he was about to chew all his nails off. "But . . . your feelings. You're unsafe!" The Shadow Man couldn't even form coherent sentences anymore. It was like Regina's panic had transferred to him—and it was too much for him to handle, it was too heavy in the infinite suit.

"Nothing can be more horrible than this!" Regina said, laughing at her own misery. "So I don't care what happens anymore. It won't be worse than this."

She started toward the door.

"You can't do this to me," the Shadow Man whispered.

Regina stopped and looked at him. He had buried his face into his palms. He didn't look like the best businessman in the two worlds at all. The mask of perfection had fallen.

"I'm sorry," she said. "Is there anything I can do?" The anxious feeling inside of her was almost her friend at this point.

"Yes, there is." The Shadow Man stood up straight and tugged on this suit. "You can stay here. In this room. Forever."

"But, you just said . . ." Regina realized there was no use talking to him. "I can't do that. I'm sorry."

The Shadow Man just stared at her motionless, his arms hanging next to him as if they were boneless. Only his mouth twitched from time to time. He then nodded ever so slowly. "Go. It's better if you leave. For everyone."

Regina knew she had to leave. Outside of the perfect room, the whole world lay. With friends and experiences not as perfect, maybe even uncomfortable or downright painful. But Regina had never liked the Shadow Man's perfect appearance anyway.

In that moment, she stopped running away from what she was feeling. Instead, she turned toward it with bravery.

Nausea still swirled around in Regina's tummy and dizziness made her head spin. The difference was that she didn't mind. On the other side of that door, her whole life lay. With all of its pain and hurt and sadness, it was still hers to live. And she was not going to hide from it. With all of its imperfections, it was perfect.

The Shadow Man lowered his head and turned away. "Leave. Now, before I change my mind." His tail hung sadly, not even making an effort to hide.

"I'm sorry." Regina placed her hand on the door's handle, but she didn't push it down. She wanted to ask the

134

Shadow Man why he was so sad. She wanted to ask him how he had gotten here. And why he didn't come with her, leaving his perfectly infinite suit behind.

"Don't be sorry. I can't stand pity."

Without even trying, the handle moved under Regina's hand, and she fell through the door, leaving the Shadow Man and the perfect room behind.

Dread's muscles popped like balloons, and Regina could almost see her fear evaporate and turn into nothing.

18 · BEHIND EVERY STRANGE FACE

Regina was standing somewhere in Dara Forest. The door she had stepped through was nowhere to be seen anymore.

The uncomfortable feelings inside of her had settled down, like she had left them all in the Tunnel.

It felt good to be standing outside. The air was clean and fresh, the trees vibrant and beautiful. Regina closed her eyes and took a deep breath. Her throat still felt dry, and there was a strange taste in her mouth—aftermaths of the Tunnel.

No one was around her. Regina wondered where Joey and Brunorth were. And with them, Mal entered her mind as well. But this time, not with fear and terror like it had inside the Tunnel.

Regina wondered where he was in his Andarian journey. Had he made it through Napharata? Had he stayed? Had he wished himself back to Losthan? And most of all: Did he remember his forgotten past?

Regina felt a strange tingling in her chest. She remembered how the boy tried to protect her from everything that wasn't even a threat. She remembered the girl who looked just like Regina, the girl with the sunshine smile—Mal's sister. That boy was not someone to fear.

But he was a child of Losthan. And all those souls had said he was the cause of all their deaths. Still, the boy Regina had gotten to know was not someone she felt like she should fear.

Regina looked up at the thin rays of sunshine sneaking in between the leaves. Believing Mal was going to hurt her, believing he was a savage child of Losthan felt wrong. After all, he was just a person. A person with feelings, likes and dreams. A person just like her. No matter where he had come from. No matter the color of his skin. No matter the unusual structure of his face.

Regina wiped the tears from her eyes. She thought she cried too often. These were not tears of sadness though—more like tears of relief, trust, a sense of belonging, understanding and love.

This moment—it felt right. Trusting. Believing. Understanding that monsters didn't hide behind every strange face; who hid there instead were simply different versions of her. Monsters were only real inside the Tunnel.

Mal was not going to hurt her. She had to believe that. She wanted to believe that. Even if it turned out to be untrue, it still seemed like a better choice to trust and love than to live in constant fear of a possible doom. To see a threat behind every strange face.

What was *strange*, after all? It was nothing more than something one's eyes were not used to. Something one's mind didn't understand. *Strange* was a way of seeing. *Strange* was only inside the eyes looking, not in the thing being looked at.

The fear she had felt inside the Tunnel, the infinite worlds swirling inside the Shadow Man's suit—it was a way of looking at the world. And Regina didn't want that endless darkness swirling around inside of her.

Right then and there, Regina decided—she wasn't going to choose fear. Behind every strange face, she would not see a threat, but a different version of herself.

Unlike the Tunnel, this feeling felt right. It lifted her up, made her smile and made her want to *live*—not hide away in a room.

It was time to find Joey, Brunorth and wait for Mal to come back. Because Regina believed that he would make it through Napharata. He would come back to Cetana. And they would be friends. Because one's past didn't matter next to the light that shone from the heart. And there was light inside Mal—she could feel it, she had seen it.

Regina heard footsteps approaching her. *That must be Joey*, she thought with a smile on her face. Every uncomfortable feeling had crawled off her like parasites unable to survive in the environment that was her.

Regina began to turn, her eyes anticipating to meet Joey's. But they never did.

Before she could see who the footsteps belonged to, a large sack swallowed her head and upper body. Whoever pulled it over her head tightened its strings around her waist, so she couldn't escape.

And just like that, all Regina's eyes could see was darkness.

19: A DEEP SORT OF KNOWING

When Regina opened her eyes, she only saw darkness. She was not standing on her feet—she felt her body lying on the hard ground. The earth was cold and moist under her. She must have blacked out.

"This is not how it was supposed to happen." Regina heard someone muttering. The voice moved—the speaker was nervously pacing. "This is not how it was supposed to happen."

Regina didn't recognize the voice. It was manic and raspy, like its speaker had been screaming and crying. The only thing Regina could conclude was that her abductor was male—a young one, since his voice was not deep yet like an adult's.

She lay there on the cold, hard ground, unable to move.

The sack's strings were tightened around her waist, pushing her arms against her sides. She felt her legs had been tied too.

She didn't want to believe it, but there was only one person who had any reason to kidnap her—the person she had tried her hardest to believe in.

So what was there to be done in a situation like this? Regina could have wished herself back home, but she was not a girl who gave up this easily.

She concentrated her attention on her breathing. She could breathe—she was not going to suffocate inside of the sack. She didn't want to think, she didn't even want to let herself realize what kind of situation she was in.

"I ruined everything." The voice faltered, and its source lowered. Regina thought the boy must have crouched on the ground. Maybe even curled up, hugging his knees close to his chest—he sounded pathetic.

Regina couldn't imagine the source of this pitiful voice hurting her. A deeper sort of knowing she couldn't have explained told her that she didn't need to be afraid.

"It will be okay," that deeper sort of knowing in Regina made her say.

141

The reaction she got was a long moment of silence and stillness. A tied up girl in a sack consoling her abductor must have taken a while to process.

"Geez, are you serious?" The boy's voice stood up and took a couple of angry steps away from Regina. His feet stomped on the ground like they wanted to punish the earth. And then he screamed. Not a frightened scream like the one people made when they saw something scary, like a ghost or a monster. This scream was the sound of someone who had had enough. Enough of life, enough of the world and enough of keeping it all in. Enough of everything.

He sounded so pathetic that Regina felt embarrassed for him.

"I'm sorry," said Regina when everything was quiet again. She used every muscle in her belly to sit up. She still didn't see anything, but she turned toward the sound of the boy. "I'm sure everything's not ruined." She was a bit scared of how the boy would react. She didn't want to say the wrong thing and set him off. "Can I . . . help?"

Regina got startled by the sudden sound right in front of her. She hadn't heard the boy approach her, and now he was so close to her, she could feel his breath through the thick

142

fabric of the sack.

"You can't help me," he said, his voice now calmer. The screaming had made it even raspier. Perhaps this was not the first time he had tried to let it all out. "No one can."

"There's always a chance to turn around." Regina's voice was a shy whisper. Like she thought anything louder than that would break the fragile boy in front of her to pieces.

A long moment of silence was his answer once again. This stillness was longer than the previous one. It was like the world had stopped around them. Every tree, every gust of wind was waiting for his reaction.

Instead of speaking, the boy moved. His arms snaked around Regina. But not in a dangerous way at all. He moved until there was no space left between them, just the thick material of the sack.

Regina's eyes opened wide. She just sat there like a little worm and let him hug her. Whoever he was. Whatever he wanted. And there was no lie in his embrace. There was no menace. Just something only that deep sort of knowing could understand.

But this honest moment couldn't last forever. The boy let go of Regina, and she felt him shaking his head ever so slightly. "It's too late for me." And then he stood up. "Everyone I ever cared about left me. And it's not even because they never loved me, I know they did. But they left me anyway. Because I'm not worth sticking around for." He took a couple steps away from Regina. "And *I* remember all of it."

Regina's stomach flipped. Not only because the boy's last sentence basically confirmed that he was Mal, but because the feeling he was talking about—Regina knew it all too well. Her father had abandoned her and never looked back after all. The feeling of not being wanted, of not being good enough for others had haunted her so deeply that it had almost made her take the hand of the Beast not so long ago.

But before she could say anything, the boy continued.

"But it doesn't matter now, it doesn't matter." His voice started to turn manic again. "Because you're here, and I won't let you go. We can stay together, and I won't lose you. I won't lose anyone ever again. Because I will never ever let you go."

20 TALK TO ME

As Regina listened to the boy's obsessed rambling, she realized that he must have been the silhouette who had been watching her in the forest all this time. He must have been waiting for a moment when she would be alone and he could carry out his plan.

Still, Regina didn't want to give in to panic. That wouldn't have solved anything.

"Wait, wait," she said, trying her hardest to make her voice calm. "What are you talking about? I don't know who you are, but I'm sure you don't have to do this for me to be your friend." Regina was almost sure she was talking to Mal, but she didn't want to let him know she was aware of his identity. She wanted to give him a chance to stay anonymous, thinking that the chances of him letting her go

145

were higher that way. "Let's start this over and you'll see that I won't leave you. I promise. I know exactly how that feels. I would never do that to anyone."

"But you did!" answered the boy between disillusioned laughs. "You are such a hypocrite, always thinking you stand up for people, but when it comes down to it, you're just like the rest of them. You leave."

"No, I'm . . ." Regina didn't know what to say. How could she take part in someone's delusions? Mal and Regina didn't know each other, no matter how hard Mal wanted to believe otherwise. He was not talking about her—it was not Regina who had left him. It was the girl who he had confused her with this entire time. The girl with the sunshine smile—Mal's sister, Ness.

"Do you . . . do you remember?" Regina attempted to find out if the boy had regained his memories, trying not to reveal she knew Mal's identity.

"Remember what?" the boy said, annoyed. "I remember everything. I'm not like you. Forgetting when it becomes inconvenient. I wouldn't even be surprised if you had forgotten about me too."

Regina's trust in herself wavered. She *was* prone to

forgetting certain memories. Was it possible that . . . she knew Mal? She had just forgotten?

If she could have moved her arms, she would have buried her face right into her palms. But she just sat there helplessly like a sack of potatoes.

"I'm sorry, I don't know what to say," she said in a dying voice. "I'm not sure what you're talking about. But what I do know is that I am here right now. And I would gladly be your friend."

After a moment of silence, the answer came in the form of a small, forced laugh. "Sure, now that you're scared out of your mind."

"I'm not scared," Regina said, her voice steady. "I'm not scared of you," she added, her voice softer. "I know you won't hurt me."

"How do you know? You think I'm that much of a wimp, right?"

"No, no, of course not, geez." Regina felt like there was no right thing to say to this boy. "I just . . . I don't know. I just feel like you won't."

"I did . . ." he said, a hint of regret in his voice, "before."

The article from Losthan came to Regina's mind. The

picture of the girl with the sunshine smile. And the news of her passing.

"You . . . you did? You really did that?"

No answer came again for a long moment. Regina felt his eyes looking at her though.

"Of course I did. What, you forgot that too?"

Regina gathered her brows. This conversation was starting to get weirder and weirder. What was Mal thinking exactly? That he was talking to his dead sister who he had killed?

"I . . . um . . . I forgive you?" she said, since she couldn't think of anything better.

"Okay," the boy answered. He started to sound like he didn't understand this conversation either. "Great." Regina could basically feel him rolling his eyes.

She sat there for a while, unable to think of anything to say. The boy must have stood motionless as well, because she didn't hear him moving.

"Let me take a look at you," he said, his voice close, and Regina felt him sitting down in front of her. "It's been a while since I've seen you."

Regina stiffened. She felt the strings loosen around her

waist and arms. It had gotten hot inside the thick sack. Her face was warm with sweat.

She felt the prickly material slide upward and over her head. As light sneaked inside, she closed her eyes.

Even when she felt cool air hitting her wet face, and her eyelids were red with light, she didn't open her eyes. She kept them shut and lowered her head.

"Why won't you look at me?" the raspy voice said, tinted with hurt.

Regina shook her head. "I don't want to. Because . . . if I don't know who you are . . . it could be like this never happened. You can go on from this."

Silence again. Then Regina heard him swallow. And soon after, a sound revealed that the boy had lain back into the grass with a sigh.

Regina positioned herself so she would be facing away from him. She felt something heavy on her feet, so when she was sure she won't see the boy, she slowly opened her eyes. A thick plant was twisted around her ankles—it looked like a bean stock. She couldn't run away, even if she wanted to—Regina didn't know what Andarian plant it might have been, but it was secure around her ankles, almost like a chain.

She pulled her knees up to her chest and hugged them. The air was comfortably cool, like always in Andara. There was no one around. It was like a little piece of this world had been carved out, just for them. Even if this situation was more than uncomfortable, Regina felt like she needed to be there. She needed to listen. She needed to understand. Before something more happened than a sack around someone's head. Before uncomfortable turned into something irreversible.

"There are so many horrible articles in Eris' castle," she said, resting her head on her knees and her eyes on the little piece of sky looking in between the trees. "I've been trying to understand more. Why these things happen. All the time. And how we can prevent them from happening. I don't know the answer. I don't think anyone does. But here, in Andara, I realized that I could be one of those people doing those horrible things. Anyone could be. Given the right circumstances. The *wrong* circumstances. It's not that hard to understand. If you're willing to listen. I'm willing to listen. Please. Talk to me."

21: KNOWING AND BELIEVING

"I'm not sure what you want to hear." The boy's voice was calmer now, though still raspy from the screaming. Regina could feel him lying comfortably in the grass behind her.

"Well, you said I left," said Regina. "I'm sure there's a lot you could tell me. You know, catching up?"

After a short silence, the boy said, "It will never be enough."

Regina waited for him to elaborate, but when he didn't, she had to ask, "What won't be enough?"

"The Asantosa."

Regina's eyes moved like she was searching for answers in the empty air in front of her. Asantosa was the glowing red liquid that flowed across Mount Napharata. People who chose to stay in its caves produced it. It was not clear exactly how, but it had been said that the discontent of Napharatians created it. This lava-like substance gave power to Lord Ate, the deified leader of Mount Napharata, while Napharatians believed the more Asantosa they produced, the more successful, better, stronger they would become.

The boy mentioning Asantosa meant that . . . Mal had chosen to stay at Napharata. Lord Ate's illusions had convinced him.

"Asan-tosa?" That was all Regina could say—Mal choosing Napharata had shocked her.

"My mom left because I wasn't good enough." The boy continued, ignoring Regina's confusion. "I have to be better, but it just feels like it will never be enough. You left too. It doesn't matter how much Asantosa I create, I will always suck. I will always suck!" The boy shouted, and the ground vibrated when he pounded his fist into it. He sounded like an angry gorilla.

Regina stiffened, but she didn't turn.

"They used to tell me my mom died because of me. Did you know?"

Regina's lips parted, but she couldn't answer.

"That she would have survived if she had something to

live for." He laughed a laugh filled with hurt.

His sister hadn't been the only one Mal had lost. He had lost his mom as well, maybe his whole family. He remembered now.

People had told him his mom had died because of him. Had they been right? Had Mal been the cause of his whole family's passing? In Losthan, such a case was not uncommon.

Was Mal really the brute child of Losthan? The aggressive behavior he had shown certainly didn't indicate otherwise. Regina didn't want to believe it, but she couldn't stop the knot from forming in her stomach.

That deep sort of knowing told her that Mal was not someone to fear. But knowing was not believing.

"They were right," the boy continued. "They were right. If she had a better son, she wouldn't have died. I basically killed her." He laughed with the pain of it all. Like the realization had not been easy. "And *you* . . . You would have stayed too if it wasn't for me."

Regina didn't know what to say, but her stomach got smaller by the minute. She tried to push the thoughts out of her head that told her this boy couldn't be trusted, that he could snap any moment and do to her what he had done to his family.

Maybe that was why he had kidnapped her—he felt like she was unfinished business.

Regina couldn't swallow the foul taste in her mouth.

"You . . . you can't change what already happened," said Regina, trying to keep her voice steady. "But you can avoid making the same mistakes." She was hoping desperately that her words would reach him. "It will all be okay if you don't keep making the same mistakes."

After a short silence, the boy said, "What you say sounds logical. But that doesn't save it from being the worst advice I've ever heard."

Regina buried her face into her palms. She had been stupid to think she could ever offer useful advice to a child of Losthan. They saw two different worlds.

"So what's your plan then?" she asked.

"I have no plan. I just wanted to be with you for a little while. Everything has gotten a little crazy."

I just wanted to be with you for a little while. These words softened the knot in Regina's stomach.

Regina didn't know what to say, so she let the boy sit

with her in silence. Perhaps that was all he needed. To feel like he was sitting with the sister he had lost. The sister with the sunshine smile.

The Dragontears on the trees began to light up. The tiny white flowers named Fairypalms moved their petals, closing up for the night. A veil of black slowly descended onto the world—the day was coming to an end.

Time passed unnoticed. Regina didn't know how long they had been sitting there. She was tired—the day had exhausted her.

She didn't want to fight it. She was glad her mind was too tired to think. She let it rest, careful not to think a thought that might wake it from its peaceful slumber.

The boy next to her didn't say anything either. His aura felt peaceful. Maybe he was letting himself rest after his exhausting day too. Maybe there were no thoughts in his head either. Maybe none were needed in that moment at all.

"I don't think I can let you go, Regina," said the boy. So his mind wasn't thought-free after all.

His thoughts would come crashing into the moment like wrecking balls.

"What . . . what do you mean?" Regina asked, the knot in

her stomach starting to form again.

"You know what I mean. I don't want anyone to know I did this. It makes me look even more of a wimp than I am."

"But I don't know who you are," said Regina, her voice almost begging. "I didn't see you, I was so careful."

"Ah, come one. Who are you trying to fool? You know perfectly well who I am."

"I didn't see you, I swear!"

"But you know nonetheless!"

Regina couldn't reply. She did believe the boy who had kidnapped her was Mal. But did she know it too?

"Don't . . . don't do anything you will regret," said Regina, trying her best to sound convincing. "You have so many regrets already."

"So what's one more?"

"No, don't!" Regina tried to crawl away on all fours like she was anticipating the boy to attack her. She couldn't get far because of the plant around her ankles.

See, you aren't safe, I told you. The Shadow Man's voice echoed inside Regina's head. *You shouldn't have left it behind. You can still take it back. Take it back.*

Before Regina could consider what he was talking about,

something appeared in front of her, pushing out everything from her head. It had jumped out of the bushes like a proud stallion—the black skeleton dog encompassed by smoke. It stood right there, in front of her, and looked at her with its hollow eyes.

"You leave her alone!" A strong voice of another young man tore across the air. It made Regina freeze and her eyes shoot open.

She knew this voice. Even though she hadn't heard it many times, she knew it undoubtedly.

Regina heard the sound of a struggle, but she still didn't turn. She stood frozen, staring into the hollow eyes of the skeleton dog.

As she tried to deduce who the two voices belonged to, two strong arms scooped her up from the ground.

"It's going to be all right," said the new voice, carrying her away from the scene, fast.

Even in the dark, Regina could see the Dragontears' warm light reflecting on the unusual creases on the bubblegum skin around his eye.

Regina looked above Mal's shoulder. They were getting farther and farther away from the dark figure who was floundering to his feet.

Regina had wanted to believe the owner of the raspy voice was Mal. But she had known. Somewhere, she had known all along who had taken her. She just didn't want to believe it.

Sometimes, when knowing and believing overlapped, they caused destruction. Like two planets colliding. Pushing, pulling and twisting each other until only one world remained, leaving no room for anything else to exist. No other possibilities, just the truth.

There it was, stumbling to his feet in the distance—the truth. Mal was not the villain trying to harm Regina—he was the hero, saving her from the villain.

The villain . . . The silhouette in the dark. Knowing and believing overlapped. Two planets collided and only one remained. This new planet, it bore the name Jasper.

22 · A SAD KIND OF CALM

Regina stared in front of herself with wide eyes, trying to piece all that had happened together while Mal carried her through the forest.

It had been Jasper. Jasper had kidnapped her.

Regina tried to think back to all the things he had said. All the things she had thought Mal was saying.

Everyone left him.

His mom died because of him.

And I left him too.

Everyone leaves him.

Because he's not worth sticking around for.

There were no more trees around them as Mal stepped out onto the Field of Cetana. The millions of stars above them were bright. How could they shine so bright when pain this deep existed?

Mal set Regina down on the grass. He took the plant around her ankles into his hands.

Regina didn't pay much attention to him. She couldn't help but think about the dark silhouette they had left behind. The dark silhouette who had been watching her from the woods. Who had kidnapped her just so he could sit with her for a little while. Regina had never thought that surrounded by that many people, someone could be this lonely.

Mal fiddled with the plant, and with one swift whack, he broke it. He pulled it from Regina's legs and threw it between the trees.

"Don't litter!" A deep voice echoed from Dara Forest.

Regina didn't even flinch at the sound. It was probably a talking tree. Or the unfriendly elf, Heathcliff, who was obsessed with keeping the forest clean and healthy.

Mal, on the other hand, stood up and hurried into the woods, after the plant.

When he emerged from the forest, plant in hand, Regina was sitting with her knees pulled up, hugging her legs. She was facing away from Mal, resting her eyes on the endless field.

All the huts seemed so little. They were like little lanterns as the Dragontears' tiny buds lit them up on the inside. The stars above them made the land look like a calming video anyone could fall asleep watching.

Even though Regina felt calm, she wasn't happy. It was more of a sad kind of calm, heavy with problems she had no power to solve.

Several minutes had passed since Regina heard Mal come out of the forest, but the boy didn't sit next to her or even approach her. Regina turned her head to see what he was doing.

Mal was leaning against a tree—a non-speaking one—and he kept rubbing his forehead with his left hand.

Regina furrowed her brows. Mal looked distressed.

Regina's mind was so full of Jasper that she hadn't even thought about what Mal had gone through. Had he completed his journey? If he had come back, he must have. Had he made it through Mount Napharata and Lord Ate's illusion? Had he regained his memories?

Who was he?

As Regina inspected Mal with her eyes, she noticed that

162

his chest was moving unnaturally fast. He *was* in distress.

Regina lifted her head. "Mal?"

No response.

"Thank you for helping me."

Regina could see now that Mal was shaking. She stood up and hurried to him, but before she could touch his shoulder, Mal pushed her hand away.

Regina saw his face now. It was drenched in sweat. His eyes were unfocused like he wasn't seeing what was in front of him, but something completely different.

"Mal, are you okay?" All Regina could do was try. "What happened to you?"

Mal's breath came in rapid, uneven gasps. "I'm so . . . angry," he said through clenched teeth.

Regina noticed herself taking half a step back.

Mal began rubbing his forehead again, his eyes squeezing shut. "I want to . . . burn . . . it all . . . down!"

Regina didn't know what was going on, but she saw something. Something shining inside Mal's pocket. And it made her feel like she could move closer to the boy.

"I know what you're feeling," she said as softly as she could.

She remembered when she had been suffering from visions of a cloaked man—Lord Ate. She knew now that it had been the little piece trying to awaken inside of her—a piece of Lord Ate that was inside every single human being.

"It will be all right, trust me. Just listen to my voice. Just my voice nothing else. You can let everything else go. Breathe with me, Mal."

When Regina was anxious, breathing techniques always helped to calm her. Jasper had often aided her with her breathing when she was having a panic attack. The memory made a lump in Regina's throat, but she continued talking to Mal, instructing him how to breathe.

Maybe Regina's appearance was not the only thing she shared with the girl with the sunshine smile. Maybe her voice rang like hers as well.

Mal's muscles slowly relaxed.

23: THEIR OWN LITTLE WORLD

"Are you feeling better?" Regina asked.

She and Mal were sitting on the ground, backs against the trunk of a tree on the edge of Dara Forest.

"Yeah. Thanks, little one."

They were both looking up at the stars. Even though the millions of stars were always visible in Andara, when night came, descending behind the many shiny dots, it was impossible not to stare up at the sky.

"That's what you called her, right? Ness?" Under the quiet stars, safely wrapped into the calm of the night, honest words could be spoken so easily.

"Yes." Mal's voice was soft with the memory of her.

"I'm sorry, Mal." Regina still didn't know exactly what had happened to Mal. But from all she had seen, she knew

165

Mal deserved her sympathy. No matter what the skull-carriers had said, no matter what those strange articles from Losthan wrote, Mal couldn't have hurt his sister. Mal couldn't have hurt anyone. Regina felt it, deep inside her bones. Only someone in the Tunnel would have believed otherwise.

"Yeah." Mal's voice was quiet. There and then, under the shelter of the night, they were not a part of the world for a little while. "I miss her so much. My little Ness." Regina could hear the sadness break through his voice. "She wasn't weak. Not in the least. She stared evil in the eye every day without ever flinching. Without ever complaining. She was just happy to be alive. With her big brother." Mal's voice faltered. He lowered his head and Regina could hear him quietly sobbing.

"I saw her, you know," said Regina, as gently as she could. "She talked to me in my dream. She said she'll always be by your side."

Mal sniffled. "Really?"

"Yes. She kept writing M+N into the dust as she talked to me."

Mal made a sound that was the combination of laughing

and crying. "I taught her that." He sniffed, trying to make his voice sound even. "I taught her how to write our names. Girls aren't allowed to study in Losthan. Only boys go to school. But I taught her some things anyway."

Regina didn't say anything. She just listened.

"She loved it when I read to her. Especially books with evil fairies. Those were her favorites. I used to read her the same book over and over. There aren't many books in Losthan. Most of them are not allowed. They don't want the people to get any ideas, you know."

Mal's voice was calmer now, he was comfortable inside his memories.

"But when we were together, we weren't children of Losthan. We made our own little world. It was just me and her. And all the hate, the violence, the injustice—it couldn't get to us. It was like it didn't even exist. Because in our own little world, there was none." Mal paused, and Regina knew his eyes were filling up with tears as the realization of his sister's loss struck him like merciless lightening.

Their own little world was no more.

"I'm . . . so sorry Mal." Regina wished she could do something to ease Mal's pain, something to bring Ness back, to give them back the peaceful place they had made for each other in a town of chaos. But she couldn't do anything besides letting him feel what he needed to feel.

"You would never hurt your sister . . ." she said softly. "But then, who did?"

"Yeah, well . . . It's not easy for me to talk about that."

"Oh, sure, no problem." Regina shook her hands defensively. "I'm sorry if I was too pushy."

"No, it's okay. You should know. After all I put you through." Mal smiled a sweet smile at Regina.

"You didn't put me through anything," said Regina in a small voice. "I was an idiot. I put myself through all of it. It's clear as day that you're a nice guy."

A hint of sadness snuck into Mal's smile. "It's not that clear what I am, really. Not even to me. But when you say it like that, it's easier for me to believe it too. You're so much like Ness. I was a nice guy in her eyes too. She used to call me her hero." Mal paused, probably waiting for his eyes to swallow their tears. "She was never very healthy, Ness. Our parents were . . . well, let's just say that they had unhealthy habits. That's why I was born like this." He gestured toward his face. "And that's why Ness was always sick. She was very weak, a fragile little thing. When she was a baby, I was scared to death that she will suddenly just . . . break. But she never did. She was much stronger than she looked." His voice faltered again, and he had to pause for a short moment to pull himself together. "But our parents' habits got worse and worse. One day, two men came dressed in black uniforms. They took us to Initiation Orphanage. This was the first time Ness met other kids. And let's just say that kindness is not that cool in Losthan. They sensed her weakness like wolves right when we walked through the door. I protected her as best I could. Gave bloody noses often. But I couldn't always be there. I had to go to school, and whenever I left her there, they would . . . do horrible things to her." His voice was uneven, and he needed a moment of silence again. "She always kept that stupid picture of me with her," he finished in a dying voice.

"That's why it was in her hands," Regina said, her eyes filled with tears. "I'm so sorry, Mal."

"Not quite purple, not quite pink, I love you more than you might think." Mal wiped his eyes. "I used to say that to her when I had to leave her. Because the picture . . . it was discolored. It had this strange color that was not quite purple . . . and not quite pink. It was her favorite color."

"I'm so sorry," Regina said again, desperate to take even just a tiny bit of Mal's pain away.

Everything Mal had kept inside broke loose. He let his tears flow as sorrowful sobs mourned the loss of the one he loved most. Who, in the end, he couldn't protect.

Regina enclosed him in a hug. Mal grabbed onto her and cried into her shoulder.

The moment lasted for a long while. Regina shared Mal's pain. Quietly, she cried with him.

24 · MORE THAN ONE LIFE

The time came when there were no more tears to shed. Mal and Regina let go of each other. Mal had calmed down, relieved from the feelings he had released.

"They blamed me for everything, of course," he said, wiping the last of his tears away. "The freak did it, he's crazy. Losthan rule enforcers knew perfectly well what happened though, so I wasn't punished. They just needed a scapegoat. And I was perfect for that. It's one thing to be a child of Losthan, but to be a child of Losthan and also look like this?" He gestured toward his face again. "Even monsters fear mutants."

"You're not a mutant," said Regina with a combination of sadness, anger and compassion swirling around inside of her.

"I know, little one," said Mal softly, putting his hand on top of Regina's head. "I know."

Regina watched the stars flickering—it was like the night was blinking with its million eyes. It must have been hard to be a child of Losthan. It was hard for Regina to grow up with parents who were constantly fighting and then watch her father leave and never look back. But at least there were places for her to hide from it all, like the library or the company of a friend. From what Regina had learned, Losthan seemed like a place where everyone was fighting, not just the parents, and not just some of the time, but all the time. The only place to hide from it all was their own little world—if they were lucky enough to have one.

Something else crossed Regina's mind too. Sometimes, people thought things about her that weren't true. For example her aunt, who Regina had only seen twice in her life, brought her dolls on her seventh birthday, but Regina had never liked to play with dolls. Not even when she was a tiny child. But Regina wasn't mad at her aunt—she must have assumed Regina liked dolls, because she was a girl. She couldn't know better when they had only met one time.

Being a child of Losthan came with its own kind of

assumptions. Not just from one's aunt, but from the whole world. But even if someone was from Losthan, they were still people. Just like two human beings from any other city in the world weren't the same, Regina was sure two people from Losthan weren't the same either.

Thinking all that through, Regina came to the conclusion that it was pretty stupid to assume anything about anyone.

"Do you have to go back there?" she asked, already knowing the answer.

Mal sighed. "There's not much left for me there. But that's where I have to go back to, I guess. Where I saw Agnitio. In the Losthan General Hospital."

"Why were you in the hospital? You don't have to talk about it if you don't want to."

"Because Initiation Orphanage burned down, and I almost died." Mal said the words with a heavy sort of sadness.

"I'm glad you got out alive," said Regina. "Wait." She slowly put two and two together. "This wasn't *that* kind of fire, was it? The shady sort that happens is Losthan? When it's in need of a new prince?"

"Yeah, well . . . It was called Initiation Orphanage for a

reason. I only realized that here though."

"What . . . do you mean?"

"They burned it down on purpose. Hoping that only one will survive. And that one will be . . ."

"The Prince of Losthan." Regina finished the sentence, shocked.

"Yeah, well . . ." Mal scratched his head. "Losthan's pretty prehistoric in a lot of ways. They believe that it's some kind of sign if only one person survives. And that person was meant to be their prince. I always found that weird."

"Oh, my gosh, Mal! You will rule over Losthan when you go back?"

"Well, it's not that simple. Theoretically, the Prince of Losthan has absolute power, but that's not really how it works. It's pretty obvious that the Highborn families control what the prince does. But we'll see what happens if the prince doesn't comply." Mal grinned at Regina.

Regina sat back. Mal would change Losthan. As she looked into his eyes, she was sure of it. "You reached the Island of Pyara, right? Otherwise, you wouldn't be here."

Mal pulled the shiny piece of crystal from his pocket. The flower Y'sis had given him was stuck to it. As he turned

174

it between his fingers, it sparkled under the stars. He smiled as he looked at it. His eyes sparkled too. "I did. Thanks to your friends."

"Thanks to Snow? And Y'sis? Really?" For some reason, Regina smiled really wide.

"And thanks to all of you. When I was lying on the floor in Mount Napharata . . . Well, I didn't know I was lying on the floor, because I was inside of an illusion, but you know what I mean. When I was there, that feeling . . . I started remembering all that has happened. My sister, how they—" Mal bit his lips for a moment, unable to finish the sentence. "I remembered that I was the only one who survived the fire. That I'm the next Prince of Losthan. And after feeling so helpless, I finally felt in control. Like I actually had some power over my garbage circumstances. As the next Prince of Losthan, I could make everybody pay for what they had done to me. For all the pain Ness had to endure. For all of it. With Napharata, I could become a strong Prince of Losthan. And I would never have to endure that kind of pain again. But then I saw this crystal. It somehow made its way into the illusion. And it had brought all of you." Mal didn't continue. Regina noticed tears in his eyes. But these were not tears of sadness like before.

"We changed your mind, huh? About Napharata." Regina looked up at the stars, smiling.

"You did," said Mal, his voice thick. "Thank you."

Right then and there, Regina understood what Agnitio had said. She and all the others—Y'sis, Snow, Pyro and Joey—had managed to save more than one life.

"I know you'll be an awesome prince Mal. You will be the prince who finally changes Losthan. It won't be the town that stands alone anymore. I'm sure of it."

Mal smiled a smile that told he didn't think it would be that easy, but if Regina believed in it this much, maybe it was possible.

"I hope so, little one."

"I'm sure Ness thinks so too."

They smiled at each other, and under the blanket of the night, there was no fear, no anger—no assumptions.

"Regina, is that you?" The familiar voice made Regina jump as if someone had pulled the cozy blanket right off her.

"Joey, I'm so sorry! I totally forgot." She turned around. Joey was walking toward her with hands in his pockets,

Brunorth marching next to him.

"It's okay. I was just about to head back. I thought maybe you might have gone back to your hut or something." Joey arrived next to her. Brunorth greeted Regina with a warm lick on her hand. "Where were you? I never saw you come out of the Tunnel."

"I came out on the other end." Regina shook her head. "It's a long story, Joey. I will tell you later, promise."

"Okay, cool." Joey shrugged. "I'm just glad you're fine. That Shadow Man was weird. Oh, hey, Mal. I didn't see you there. Are you done with your journey? And you came back? That's awesome!" Joey stepped in front of Mal and offered him a high-five, so Mal slammed his palm into his.

"Thanks, Joey. It's good to be back."

Joey sat down next to them, and the blanket of the night was covering all three of them now. They talked about meaningless and not so meaningless things until the sun started peeking out at the edge of the land. When the sun rose, it looked over the world to see what had changed since it had last seen it the previous day. Regina could have sworn that on this day, she saw the sun smile.

25. SHADOW SPILL

Regina, Mal, Joey and Brunorth stood up at the edge of Dara Forest when the sun covered the land with light. The grass of the Field of Cetana seemed greener than before. The sun felt more comfortable on Regina's skin. And the air had no weight on her shoulders.

As they walked through the Field of Cetana, they noticed someone standing in the distance, on the side of the field where there were no huts. Right when Regina saw him, a little bubble of joy burst somewhere inside of her. The warm brown figure stood there calmly like it was beckoning them. They made their way toward it. As they got closer, they realized it was Agnitio. The smile on his face was even wider than usual as he looked down at them.

"How nice to see you all," he said. "Mal, I'm glad you

made it back."

"I'm glad too," said Mal. "I remember it all now. Thank you for bringing me here from the hospital. I don't know what I would have done if I just woke up there . . . alone and without any memories." Mal nodded to himself. "Thanks, Agnitio."

"It's yourself you need to thank, Mal. I am merely an opportunity. It is you who chose to take it."

Mal nodded with a smile, appreciating the faun's words. "So, um, how about that tea?"

Agnitio smiled and without a word, he turned around and walked to his hut, Regina, Mal, Joey and Brunorth following him.

Once they sat at Agnitio's wooden table, the faun started brewing them some Nangrass tea. The fat root was fussy as he took the skin it had shed, but the faun could calm it down with the sound of his voice.

As he placed the cups of tea in front of Regina, Mal and Joey, he turned to Regina and said, "So you've met the Shadow Man."

Regina looked at Agnitio, surprised, and just when she was about to ask how he knew, she realized that the faun probably knew more about them than anyone else.

"Yes," said Regina, lowering her head in shame. She wasn't proud of how she had acted in the Tunnel. Her tea was still translucent.

"Joey, for you it was like a walk in the park," said Agnitio with a little laugh.

Joey shrugged with a grin. "It's not a big deal." His tea started to turn pistachio green, just like the shirt he was wearing. Regina suspected it might have been his favorite color.

"You have your own fights the Shadow Man can't get to." Agnitio placed his hand on Joey's shoulder for a long moment.

Joey nodded, a hint of seriousness on his face. Regina wondered what fights Joey had to fight. He always seemed so calm and collected. Maybe there were some things inside of him he never talked about.

"Who is that guy anyway?" Regina asked. "Is he a Living Dead too?"

"No," said Agnitio, placing his hands behind his back, wondering. "He was never human. He's an Andarian creature, just like Astraea, Ate or me."

"Really?" Regina gathered her brows. "Aren't Andarian creatures supposed to do something? Like Y'sis guards the souls, you bring the people here, and Ate and Astraea work on the balance. But the Shadow Man just . . . scares people. And himself."

Agnitio considered that for a moment. "I wouldn't say Andarian creatures are supposed to do something. This world came to be with the very first human. And all the Andarian creatures were created by . . . well, you. Humans. It's not always the most logical, but"—Agnitio shrugged— "those are humans for you." He smiled.

"So what created the Shadow Man . . . exactly?" asked Joey.

"Humans are very unique—they are the only species who can get scared by their own thoughts. They can think they are in danger when, in reality, they are not. That need to be safe in such a situation created the Shadow Man. Fears arise in humans, and they have to deal with them one way or another. They can either believe their fear, keep it, hold it close without ever really looking it in the eye, or they can turn toward it, walk through it and let it go. There's no way around fear, only through. Being willing to experience the darkness is a wonderful thing. And if that happens, fear evaporates like water, leaving nothing behind. It's a clean process. But if someone turns away from fear, it latches on to them like a parasite. That's a messier situation. That person will continuously produce waste that the Shadow Man has to collect."

"So, basically," said Joey, "he's the Andarian garbage man?"

"That's one way to put it," said Agnitio. "As you could see, he has his own ideas about who he is. It's not easy to accept that you were created to be the . . . "Agnitio scratched his horn. "Well, the Andarian garbage man, as you put it."

"So what he has inside his suit is not valuable after all," Regina thought aloud. "It's trash."

"Darkness is a powerful kind of waste," said Agnitio. "And it didn't take long for the Shadow Man to get addicted to its power." He shook his head. "But it's not easy— carrying around all that darkness. It's not easy at all. These two opposites—the need for darkness' power and the wanting to be free from its weight—are in a constant battle inside of him. Darkness is very heavy, but so tempting at the same time."

"That doesn't sound very pleasant," said Mal.

"It doesn't, does it?" said Agnitio.

Regina felt a strange sadness wash over her. She remembered how horrible it felt to be in the Tunnel. She knew now that she had made that feeling evaporate when she pushed the handle down and fell out the perfect door. But the Shadow Man couldn't leave all that darkness behind. And it was not just one person's fears he had to carry, but the waste of every single person's fears since the beginning of time. Regina couldn't even imagine how that must have felt like. How heavy that suit must have been.

"How could we help him?" asked Regina, hoping they could do something for the Shadow Man.

Agnitio smiled. "You can help him by cleaning up after yourself. If you are willing to walk into your fear yourself, the Shadow Man doesn't have to. You won't produce waste and there will be nothing for the Shadow Man to carry." Agnitio looked up, wondering. "Wouldn't that be grand?"

Cup in hand, Agnitio turned and looked out the window of his hut, his face turned serious. "But that's not how things are. And there was a time when the suit became too heavy for the Shadow Man to carry. You can think of it like pollution—much like when people pour waste into the ocean. When all the darkness became too much for the Shadow Man, a sort of shadow spill occurred—and a significant amount of darkness poured into the other world."

"You mean the normal world?" asked Regina.

"Our world?" said Joey.

Mal sat in silence, listening to Agnitio carefully.

"Yes," said the faun, his voice grave. "And it was not without consequence." He turned toward them. "It tainted a large group of humans. Because of it, these humans were shunned by the others. They were forced out of every group, every city, every country. So they created a town for themselves. A town that stood alone."

"Losthan." Mal's voice was a stunned whisper.

Regina and Joey couldn't even speak, they sat with jaws dropped.

"Losthan," Agnitio confirmed and sat down across the table from them.

"The Corruptors . . ." was all Joey could say.

"Are the Invisible Demons the children of Losthan have

to walk with because of the shadow spill," said Agnitio, finishing Joey's sentence.

Regina looked at Mal. His face was hard from the shock. He stared at the faun with unblinking eyes.

"What does this mean?" Mal managed to ask.

"Honestly, Mal?" Agnitio took a sip of his tea. "Nothing. It means absolutely nothing."

"But all that darkness . . ." said Mal.

"Every human walks with some kind of darkness," said Agnitio. "You don't know how powerful you are. All of you, humans. There's no darkness you couldn't light up." Agnitio moved his head, gesturing toward Mal's cup of tea.

They all looked at the liquid in front of Mal—instead of being a black and white swirl like last time, it was white with only a couple of black dots.

"Nangrass never lies," Agnitio said with a smile. "It's not what you're given that matters. It's what you do with it." He took another sip of his tea.

Regina glanced at Mal, afraid of how he was taking this news. The boy was looking at his tea—and he was smiling.

26 THE MAN WHO STOOD ALONE

After drinking their cups of Nangrass tea, everybody seemed to settle down. Regina's had turned into a tiny blue ocean with waves.

They thanked the faun for everything and stood up to leave. Regina stayed behind after Joey and Mal left the hut.

"Agnitio," Regina said, "can I ask you a question?"

"Sure you can." The faun stopped washing the cups and turned his full attention to her.

"It's about the Tunnel. Why do skull-carriers and Fyes always appear in the Tunnel? Does that mean they're stuck there?" Regina hated the idea that everyone got stuck inside the Tunnel after death.

"Oh, no, no," said Agnitio, laughing a little. "It's quite the opposite, actually."

"The opposite?"

"Yes. You see, death is what humans fear the most. Fear of death is the very reason some get stuck inside the Tunnel. And all people visit the Tunnel at least once because of their fear of death. It's natural. To fear death." Agnitio smiled at Regina, making the weight of his words lighter. "But like all things, death is not as scary as humans think. But they can only understand that after they die. So after death, they celebrate. They celebrate having gone through what scared them the most. And after one goes through that, there is no more fear. The Tunnel cannot affect them anymore. They are there to enjoy that feeling of being without fear at the very place that scared them the most. Am I making sense?"

Regina nodded. Even though she didn't understand fully, Agnitio's words managed to ease her mind. "Yes. Thank you, Agnitio." She smiled at the faun.

She turned to leave the hut, but before she reached the door, she turned back around. "Oh, and there's one more thing." She reached into her pocket and pulled out the chillingly cold card the Shadow Man had given her. "Can I throw this away?"

Agnitio smiled. "There's no use in throwing it away.

That card always manages to find its way back. Every human carries it in their pocket, whether they are aware of it or not. I would keep it around. As a reminder who not to call for help." Agnitio winked.

"Okay, thank you," said Regina and slid the card back into her pocket. "Thanks for everything, again, Agnitio."

"No need to thank me. It's my pleasure." Agnitio put the last cup back on the shelf. "And Regina, I'm very proud of you. For the bravery you have shown in the Tunnel."

Regina blushed, thinking she had done absolutely nothing to be proud of.

"It takes a lot of courage to go into the darkness outside, but it takes a whole lot more to go into the darkness inside," said Agnitio. "But at the end of every trip into the dark, there's an invaluable treasure. I'm sure you would agree."

Regina nodded, a bit embarrassed.

"All right, I think I'll be going too. I'll visit the Shadow Man. Offer him some tea. He never wants it, but it's worth a try, don't you think?"

The faun and Regina left the hut together. Joey, Mal and Brunorth were waiting for her outside. The faun waved at them then placed his hands behind his back and began leisurely walking away.

As Regina watched him, she wondered where he would get the tea, since he didn't have any in his hands. Maybe he always had a couple of teacups full of tea in his robe somewhere. Or he could just magically make them appear out of nowhere.

Nonetheless, it was nice of him to offer tea to the Shadow Man—the man who had to bear all that darkness humans littered Andara with.

Regina couldn't help but feel bad for him. He scared her, because she associated him with the feelings she had felt inside the Tunnel. But still, she felt sorry for him—he had to carry all that heavy darkness by himself. Did he deserve this existence? Or was that just the way things were?

Was Losthan his fault, or were humans responsible for it by littering the world with darkness?

Regina didn't know. But she knew she didn't want to litter the world with darkness. But many probably did.

She felt sad for the Shadow Man. He was not the best businessman in the two worlds. He was the man who stood alone, dressed in a perfect, but very, very heavy suit.

27. WHAT MAKES US GOOD

After Agnitio disappeared between the trees of Dara Forest with or without his cups of tea, Regina, Joey, Mal and Brunorth made their way toward their huts.

On the way, they bumped into Snow and Pyro, who were happy to see that Mal had made it back. Especially Snow was ecstatic. When Mal thanked her for giving him the piece of crystal, she could barely hold back her tears.

They decided to get some food from their huts and have a little picnic by the ocean. Snow and Pyro were eager to hear what adventures they had had.

Neither Regina nor Mal spoke about Jasper—almost as if they had a silent agreement. She didn't want to let the others know his misdeeds for the same reason she hadn't wanted to look at her kidnapper. So if Jasper came back to them one day, it could be like they had never happened.

Whenever Jasper popped into Regina's mind, his sad silhouette she had left in the forest, she could feel her heart hurt inside of her chest. But she couldn't let herself believe that Jasper would stay that way—it was only a temporary phase for him, a momentary lapse. He would return one day with his head back on straight again. Regina believed that. She had to.

"Wow, the Shadow Man," Snow pondered. "He really is something. I mean, I feel really bad for him, but he's still like . . . scaring people, right?" She shook her head. "That's just horrible."

"The worst villains are the most pathetic if you get to know their stories," said Pyro.

"Do you think we will meet him too?" asked Snow, scared and excited at the same time.

Regina shrugged. "You could. I think you're especially likely to run into him if you are dealing with something. If you produce a lot of darkness waste or whatever."

"Then I'll probably meet him," said Mal. "I'm basically his son or something." He laughed uncomfortably.

They all looked at him, not knowing what to say. They

were all familiar with his story now, Mal had told all of them what had happened to him. There were little details of his story he had only told Regina though, which made her feel like she had a special connection with the boy.

"So, will you be able to do what you want to do?" said Pyro. "Being a new kind of Prince to Losthan. I mean, it probably won't be easy."

Snow kicked his ankle.

"What?" said Pyro. "It's the reality of it."

"What you believe, you can achieve," said Snow, offering Mal a smile.

Mal scratched his head. "Yeah, it won't be easy. But hey, I'm the Prince of Losthan, so I can do what I want." He smiled.

"So what are your plans, your majesty?" asked Joey.

Mal laughed. "Well, I'm not exactly sure yet," he said. "I just want to end the suffering of the people. Instead of adding to it like all the other princes have done so far. It's pretty obvious now that we were taught a lot of stuff in school because they knew the next prince will be one of us. We learned about how to oppress people so they'll do what you want them to do and things like that. Like, the class was literally called Oppression. But I never really agreed with any of it. I didn't say anything though. I never had to use it in real life, you know, so I didn't care." He scratched his head again. "I guess they were hoping the next Prince of Losthan would be an obedient student."

"Wow, that's crazy, Mal," said Regina. "That means that they were basically trying to brainwash you, but they couldn't. They tried to teach you to be someone, but you didn't become that person. Even though you grew up in Losthan and was taught all these things . . . Something inside you knew better."

"That's actually pretty awesome, dude," said Pyro. "I think I would be a raging maniac by now, honestly." He scratched his head too. "A lot less was enough to set me off."

Regina noticed Brunorth staring at his own tail. The dragon was sitting, his tail curled around him, and he kept tilting his head left and right as he gazed at the tip of his tail.

Regina narrowed her eyes—the dragon's tail was covered in almost unnoticeable fog. It was like white smoke was dancing around it. And then Regina saw it.

A white creature was playing with Brunorth's tail like a

little puppy with a toy. In fact, it *was* a little puppy—the skeleton of it, at least—white, encompassed by white smoke. Only a few black spots adorned the white bones, as if it were a Dalmatian skeleton. The playful creature flickered in and out of Regina's sight like a broken light bulb. Still, Regina smiled, for she knew what its presence meant.

"What makes someone good?" asked Snow, wondering.

"Even in the most extreme circumstances?" Regina continued the thought, still smiling.

All of them thought about that for a long moment, but before anyone could come up with an answer, a glowing orb appeared above them and descended right onto Mal's head. It was a strange color somewhere between pink and purple.

"What's this?" Mal said, taking it off his head.

The orb sat calmly in his hand. Mal looked at it without saying a word.

Regina turned around to see if Y'sis was nearby, but she was nowhere to be seen. She had kept her promise.

"Not quite purple, not quite pink, I love you more than you might think," said Mal, smiling, his voice soft.

Regina covered her mouth with her hands, tears filling her eyes.

Mal didn't take his eyes off the orb in his hands. His smile was calm, peaceful. He held the orb gently—as if it were the most valuable treasure in the two worlds.

"I think it's love that makes us good," he said. "I think it's love that makes us good."

CONTENTS

www.ingramcontent.com/pod-product-compliance
Lightning Source LLC
Chambersburg PA
CBHW021039130626
46552CB00005B/1919